KU-687-847

ROCKING HORSE WAR

LARI DON
ROCKING HORSE WAR

Kelpies

To Mirren and Gowan, my two top heroines, who inspired this one by demanding a quick story about horses, and got an entire novel!

Kelpies is an imprint of Floris Books

First published in 2010 by Floris Books

© 2010 Lari Don

Lari Don has asserted her right under the
Copyright, Designs and Patents Act 1988
to be identified as the Author of this Work.

All rights reserved. No part of this book may be
reproduced without the prior permission of
Floris Books, 15 Harrison Gardens, Edinburgh
www.florisbooks.co.uk

The publisher acknowledges a Lottery grant from
the Scottish Arts Council towards the publication
of this series.

The paper and board used in this paperback are
natural recyclable products made from wood grown
in sustainable forests. The manufacturing processes
conform to the environmental regulations of the
country of origin.

British Library CIP Data available
ISBN 978-086315-758-5
Printed in Great Britain by JF Print Ltd

Chapter 1

The triplets were stolen on a sunny Monday morning.

Pearl ran upstairs to call them for breakfast. She'd heard her sisters and brother singing one of their made-up nonsense songs just a few minutes before, but now the schoolroom was empty.

Surely they were too old to be playing hide and seek with her? She glanced between the school desks, behind the piano and under the kilts in the dressing-up chest.

"Emerald! Ruby! Jasper! Come out! I'm not in the mood for games. I don't want to spend all day chasing after you."

There were no toes poking out under the red velvet curtains, but Pearl stomped over to the windows to punch at them anyway, and saw that the middle window was wide open.

She sighed. The triplets weren't trying to fly again, were they? She was tired of building steps out of chests of drawers, or bumping long ladders through narrow corridors, to fetch the triplets down from impossible places before anyone noticed.

She glanced up at the sky first to check it was empty. Just a couple of swans, no truant triplets. Pearl shook her head. She didn't really expect to see her brother and sisters flying. There must be a rational explanation for their habit of appearing on top of unclimbable trees and locked buildings.

Then she looked down at the ground. The triplets weren't there either. The lawn, three floors below, led to the rockery and the garden wall, then to the woods, moors and mountains beyond. But the smooth grass was torn, clods of dark earth clustered around a pattern of round holes and deep gashes. Had the triplets jumped down, hitting the ground so hard they'd ripped into the grass when they landed?

The trail of damage continued across the lawn, not towards the northern mountains which Pearl had climbed with Father, but towards the southern ones which Mother had forbidden anyone to approach.

Pearl considered jumping straight out of the window to follow the triplets. But even if they had stayed on their feet after such a long leap, she would probably break her legs, so she decided to run down the stairs instead.

As she swung round, her big toe banged against a hard object. She bent down to rub the pain away, and suddenly noticed six long pieces of wood lying flat on the floor round the open window. Each one was shaped in a smooth curve like the cavalry sabre on Father's study wall. The wood was dark and varnished, but towards the ends of each curve were scars: round patches of wood, paler, unvarnished, splintered. Scars where something had been torn off.

Then Pearl recognised the wooden shapes. They were the rockers from the triplets' rocking horses.

Their beautiful wooden rocking horses, with jewelled bridles, leather saddles and real horsehair manes and tails. Emmie always said they looked like warriors' horses, chargers from the age of chivalry, with their flared nostrils, bared teeth and sharp hooves.

The horses had been a gift on the triplets' fourth birthday. No one knew who'd sent them, though Mother had ransacked the house for the missing gift tags.

Even at the age of ten, far too old to play with their other wooden toys, the triplets still rode their rocking horses every morning. They galloped off on imaginary quests Pearl couldn't join, because her tatty brown horse was too short for her twelve-year-old legs. But as the triplets' legs grew, their horses seemed to grow with them. Pearl had mentioned this to Father once, and he had chuckled, "Everything seems to change size as you grow up, dear girl. Wooden horses don't really grow."

She touched the splinters on the nearest curve of wood. The horses' legs had been wrenched free of the rockers, and the horses had vanished too.

Pearl stood up and looked out of the window at the hacked holes slashing away across the grass.

Hoofprints.

The triplets and the rocking horses had disappeared together.

But had the triplets taken the horses? Or had the horses taken the triplets?

Pearl frowned. Whatever daft or dangerous nonsense the triplets were up to this time, she had to find them before Mother realised they'd gone. So she jumped over the rockers and sprinted out of the schoolroom.

As she hurtled down the main stairs into the entrance hall, she passed the new Chayne family portrait, finished just last month. She stuck her tongue out at it. The artist had been so enthusiastic about painting the triplets. "Classically perfect," he'd called them, with their golden curls, green eyes, clear skin and sincere smiles on demand.

The artist was told of their angelic voices, so he'd put sheet music in their hands. But the triplets never bothered to read music, they just sang new tunes suddenly in harmony with each other, while Pearl struggled with her scales on the piano.

No one could suggest an artistic accomplishment for Pearl, so when she stood in front of his easel, the painter asked her to clutch a new illustrated geology textbook. Then he sketched her at the back of the picture, brown plaits and scowling face in the shadows of the triplets' brilliance. She would have preferred not to be in the painting at all.

Her running slowed as she reached the bottom of the stairs. Why was she bothering to chase the triplets? If they wanted to get into trouble, perhaps she should let them. She glanced back up at the portrait. Ruby and Jasper simpered at her; Emerald twinkled.

She slithered to a stop on the hall tiles. The triplets were probably off having an adventure together. But if she didn't follow them, she'd have to listen to Mother worry about them all the way through breakfast.

"Weren't you fetching the triplets for me, Pearl?" Her mother's quiet voice startled her. Pearl spun round to face the pale figure in the dining room doorway.

"They're up already, Mother, and ... em ... we're going out for a picnic breakfast. Emmie's idea. She packed the baskets last night."

"Going *out*? Not going far, I hope."

Mother's fingers were already twitching. She hated not knowing where the triplets were. She got nervous when they left the house and frantic if they were out of sight of the windows. She never seemed bothered about where Pearl went, which was usually very convenient.

"You will stay with them, won't you? Look after them? Bring them home?"

"Of course. I'm following them right now. We'll be back when we run out of food."

Pearl turned and stepped out of the front door.

Behind her, she heard Mother wrench open the nearest cupboard. Mother always tidied when she was worried about the triplets. She would dust and sweep as if she could find her missing children on the mantelpiece, behind old photos of her eldest son in uniform, or in the shoe cupboard, reflected in the polished toes and heels of the family's boots.

If Pearl took too long to find the triplets, Mother would empty drawers and bookcases, rearrange pictures, and move furniture from room to room. It would be the cleanest, neatest house in Scotland, but no one would be able to find anything for weeks.

Pearl dashed to the stables, hoping the groom had already brought her bay pony in from the field. She saw Conker's dark tail flick at the entrance to his loose box, so she saddled him as fast as she could, then leapt on his back.

Pearl trotted her pony round to the south lawn, feeling his strong warm muscles stretch as he enjoyed the morning air. Much better than riding on a cold wooden horse.

But when Conker reached the churned-up grass below the schoolroom window, he stopped so abruptly that Pearl crashed forward onto his neck.

"Walk on," Pearl ordered. But he backed away, shying at the hoofprints, shaking his dark brown mane.

"Come on, let's have an adventure, searching for those precious triplets and their mighty steeds. Walk on, boy." She clicked her tongue and urged him on with her hands and legs, but the pony refused to follow the trail.

Pearl grunted in frustration. She considered getting off and leading him, or using the crop and forcing him. But Conker was even more stubborn than she was, and she was in a hurry, so she loosened the reins and let him gallop the short distance back to the stables. She put him in his box, and took off his saddle and bridle.

"If you won't take me, I'll just have to go on my own two feet," she murmured, looking around for a treat to distract him from his fright.

She stuck a hand in the biggest pocket of the old-fashioned navy pinafore hanging up on a nail. Pearl wore it for expeditions and experiments, so its deep pockets were filled with string and pencils and other useful things. There was usually leftover food too. She found a slightly chewed carrot and offered it to Conker.

Then she tugged the old pinafore over her grey dress. Today already felt like an expedition.

Pearl sprinted from the stables to the damaged lawn. She looked up at the open window, the red velvet hanging limp on the sill. Then she turned her back on the house and followed the rocking horse hoofprints.

Chapter 2

The hoofprints were clear and stark in the bright morning light. As she ran beside them, Pearl took note of how hard the hooves had hit the ground, and how far apart the three sets of prints were. The rocking horses must have galloped along three abreast. But even at a gallop, the strides were long for toy ponies. And they seemed to be getting longer.

Had the horses been growing as they galloped away with Ruby, Jasper and Emmie?

The last time Pearl had tracked the triplets Mother hadn't known they were gone, so there had been no rush. They'd left a trail of bent nettles, torn docken leaves and broken daisy chains, which even a city tourist could have followed. Pearl had found them singing nonsense rhymes round a bush in the woods, claiming they were trying to ripen berries for tea.

Pearl followed the hoofprints to the rockery. Hardly any flowers grew there; it was a heap of spiky rocks rising out of the earth, selected and arranged to look like the Swiss Alps. The gardener often told Pearl how her older brother and his best friend had built the rock garden as a joke one summer, when she was a baby, to remind them of a holiday spent skiing and climbing.

Both boys were killed the next spring in the trenches of France. Pearl knew no one would ever knock down their folly and build a more practical rockery.

Pearl paused and looked up from the summits of the rockery to the real mountains surrounding the house. The mountains to the north she knew well, because Father was an old school friend of the family who owned them, so the Chaynes had permission to climb and track and hunt on them whenever they liked.

But the mountains to the south she only knew from her older brother's maps, because for as long as Pearl could remember, Mother had forbidden any of the family to go out of the southern gate. Mother's only explanation for this unbreakable family rule was that the neighbours to the south were unfriendly, unpredictable and best left alone.

Pearl smiled cautiously when she saw that the horses had hurdled the Alps, then kept going towards the gate in the south wall. Perhaps the triplets' escape was her chance, at last, to explore the southern lands.

Then her smile faded. She might walk the southern moors today, but she might never climb the northern mountains with Father again.

Last night, she had been running downstairs to show Father a map she'd drawn of the River Stane's source, when she'd heard his voice booming out of the study.

"Everyone lost someone in the war, Beryl. Everyone! The rest of the country is just getting on with life. It was more than ten years ago. You can't stay cooped up here for ever."

Father's courtroom lawyer voice had carried up the stairs; Mother's answering voice had faded away into nothing. As Pearl had dithered on the cold steps, wondering if she should come back later, she'd heard Father speak again.

"You can't keep the triplets cooped up for ever either. You can't keep babying them. It isn't healthy. They should be roaming the moors and mountains, like Pearl. And they should all be going off to school this year, rather than exhausting another poor tutor. It's time they grew up."

Mother's voice had risen like a bird, and Pearl had been drawn down a couple of steps to hear it.

"If we're talking about growing up, John, then you have to realise that Pearl is growing up too. She's growing into a young woman. You can't keep dragging her through boggy moors and up rockfaces as if she were a boy."

Father had snapped back, "If you would let me take Jasper out, then I wouldn't need to take Pearl. Let him act like a boy his age, then perhaps I would leave Pearl at home."

Pearl had turned back to her room, the map hanging from her fist, crushed. She hadn't bothered to show it to Father early this morning before he drove off to his week's work in Perth Sheriff Court.

She could still hear his words as she stared at the mountains. The hours lying side by side in the heather watching deer. The days scrambling on the rocks and cliffs of the Axehead and the Rhymer on the northern ridge. Not because Father enjoyed her questions and her company, but because his son was still at home riding rocking horses and singing with his sisters.

If Father didn't want to climb with her in the northern mountains, then she would use Peter's maps to get to know the southern mountains, whatever Mother said about the neighbours.

Pearl strode round the rock garden, following the hoofprints towards the high wall which separated the Chayne grounds from their neighbours' woods and moors.

Ahead of her, the three lines of prints merged into a confusion of hooves; the horses had gone single file through the gateway.

The spiked metal gate had been left open. Of course. When did the triplets ever close a door behind them?

Pearl blinked. The gateway had been empty a moment ago, but now someone was blocking her way through. Between the gateposts, polished black boots astride the line of hoof marks, stood a tall boy.

As Pearl walked briskly nearer, she could see he was dressed for hunting: tweed jacket, white shirt, red waistcoat, dark trousers and tall riding boots, all perfectly fitted and cleaned, not baggy and patched like her own outdoor clothes. He had no hat on, so his curly black hair flopped over his forehead.

Her stride faltered when she noticed he was gripping a silver rifle under his left arm and twirling a long stick in his right hand.

He smiled broadly at Pearl as she walked

towards him. He was no more than a year or two older than her, but he was a head taller.

Pearl shoved her hair out of her eyes, then realised she'd probably smeared dust from the stables all over her face. At least it would cover the freckles.

She stopped a couple of steps in front of the boy. "Good morning. Were you here when my sisters and brother rode through? Did you see which way they went?"

"I was not *here*, no." He stamped his heel into the earth between the gateposts. "Had I been *here* when someone rode through, I should have been trampled."

"Of course. But did you see them? Three blond children riding … em …" Riding rocking horses? She wasn't going to admit her fanciful suspicion to this patronising boy.

"Three blond children riding what?" He grinned like he would eat every one of her silly questions.

"Three blond children riding three horses."

"What kind of horses?"

Pearl shut her eyes briefly and pictured the triplets' rocking horses. "A chestnut stallion, and two mares: one white, one palomino. Did you see them?"

"I'm afraid I got here just a moment ago. They must have passed through before that."

"Well, thanks for all your help, but now I have to go and call them in for breakfast."

She stepped closer to the shiny bars of the gate, closer to the boy and the twirling stick.

The gnarled staff was longer than a walking

stick, and made of very dark wood, as if it had been charred or rubbed with soot before it was varnished. And it was blocking her path.

"Excuse me, please."

The stick kept swinging, circles and figures of eights and straight swipes slicing the air, as the long fingers of the boy's right hand twisted and shifted their grip.

"Aren't you too young to be leaving the garden by yourself?" he asked. "It might be dangerous."

"I'll be fine, thanks. I'm used to walking the moors and mountains to the north. I know the land."

"Do you? Do you really know the land?" His wide smile faded, and his brown eyes looked at her seriously. His still face looked like a statue she had once tried to sketch in the art gallery in Edinburgh, with its straight nose and smooth cheeks.

She answered confidently. "Even if I've never walked this land before, I'll be able to read it, and the animals and people who've crossed it, like you can read a book."

He smiled again. "Will you really? Perhaps the people who know the woods, moors and mountains best are those who listen rather than look."

Pearl snorted. There was no point in arguing. She just needed to get through the gate. "Let me past, please. I have to find the triplets, and you've no reason to stop me."

"No. I will not let you past. This is not a good day for you to leave the quiet safety of your family's grounds."

Pearl glanced up at the sky to hide her irritation.

"The weather's fair, it's hours until dusk, I'll be fine. Don't worry about me."

"There are clouds over the mountains."

She looked over, and saw grey wisps swirling round the rocky tops of the southern mountains.

She laughed. "There's not a lot of rain in those."

He laughed too. "You're right. There's no rain at all in those clouds."

She squinted at the clouds. Did they look more like smoke? Surely not, there was nothing to burn at the summits. She looked at the boy again. Was he one of the neighbours Mother was so worried about?

"May I ask your name?"

"You may ask, but I can't be bothered telling it to someone so small and insignificant." He shrugged slowly, a ripple of contempt sliding down from his shoulders.

Pearl stared at him, amazed at his ability to say the rudest things with the most glittering smiles. He gave the impression that it was a gentle joke, it meant no harm, that a good sport would take it all in good heart.

But Pearl wasn't feeling like a good sport this morning, and this boy was standing between her and the triplets. However, she needed to know more about him before she decided whether to fight back.

"What are you hunting? You're carrying a rifle, not a shotgun, so you can't be shooting grouse or pheasant, and you're dressed too smartly to be stalking deer."

"What I'm hunting, I won't shoot, unless I have to. But the gun is for swans, if I see any."

"You can't shoot swans! Isn't it illegal?"

He chuckled. "It may be illegal, but it's often wise. I prefer wisdom to obedience, don't you?"

So Pearl made what she hoped was a wise decision.

That dark stick whistling between the gateposts left no space to push past this boy. He wasn't going to be moved by argument or force, and she never bothered trying to charm people, because she didn't have the triplets' skill.

So Pearl gave up.

"Alright. As you're clearly so much older and wiser than me, I'll take your advice and go home to help Mother clear out cupboards."

"Very sensible. I hope your housework is as successful as my hunting."

"I hope so too."

Pearl trudged off, head down, looking defeated and confused, until she was on the other side of the rockery.

Then she stopped. The highest Alps blocked the view from the gate to the house, so the tall boy couldn't see whether she was still walking home.

Pearl heard him laugh. Perhaps he found it amusing to win an easy victory over a weak opponent.

She waited a moment, then dropped to the ground, slid to the edge of the rockery and looked round the foothills of the Alps.

He was still in the gateway, leaning casually against the gatepost, twirling that stick. He looked at his wristwatch, brought the stick gently to rest, pulled the gate shut and stepped to the side, behind the wall.

Then Pearl heard him start to sing: a low gentle chant, in long soft syllables which were almost words. Like the nonsense songs the triplets were always inventing, but with proper verses rather than repetitive nursery rhymes.

As the sound rose, she saw a wash of colour rise up the gate, a gritty red brown blooming up and over the black metal. From this distance, it looked like rust, but surely it couldn't be, not so fast?

When the singing stopped, Pearl counted to a hundred then ran up and pushed at the gate. It was stuck solid. The lock and latch were rusted to the frame. It would take the strength of a horse to shove it open. She couldn't climb over either, because of the long sharp spikes along the top.

How had the gate corroded so badly in such a short time? It had been fine when she stood here ten minutes ago.

She kicked the gatepost. She wouldn't reach the southern lands through this gate today. But she was still determined to leave the garden. Because now it wasn't just Mother who was worried about the triplets being out of sight.

Chapter 3

Pearl sprinted to the old orchard, where bent apple and pear trees grew right up to the high wall. Pearl and the triplets often climbed these trees, so Pearl's pleated skirt and lacing boots weren't a hindrance, as she clambered quickly up the biggest apple tree.

She scrambled from its branches to the top of the wall, and balanced there, arms open wide to the southern lands. The mountains looked closer already.

She glanced to her right. There was no one standing beside the gate. So she dangled down from the top of the wall and let go, landing with a thump on new unexplored land.

She searched for the trail of hoofprints, and found faint marks among the tall grass leading to the pheasant wood. She smiled with relief when she identified three different sets of hooves. She was still tracking three horses and three triplets.

Suddenly Pearl heard a deep thrumming above the wood. Two magnificent white swans flew overhead, their long necks pointing towards the River Stane, their massive wings drumming the air.

She made a swift wish that the arrogant boy with the stick wouldn't get them within range of his rifle, then ran into the wood.

This pheasant wood wasn't truly wild or natural. Just like the woods Pearl knew to the north, it was tended by the neighbours' gamekeepers as a shelter for pheasants, to keep them safe and happy until the autumn shooting season.

She followed the hoofmarks along a path just wide enough for horses to trot single file, past glowing silver birches, hunched hawthorns and tall smooth beeches.

As she ran, she noticed bootprints mixed in with the hoofprints, and hoped she was wrong about who they belonged to.

Then, by a massive chestnut tree, the path split into three. And so did the line of hoofprints.

Pearl slid to a stop. The triplets never split up. Why had they gone in different directions this morning? And which triplet should Pearl follow?

She spun round, looking at each path in turn. The widest path led further into the dimness of the trees, the narrowest path curved up towards the moorland, and the third path led down towards the River Stane, which flowed round the foot of the mountains.

Pearl crouched down to examine the prints. Father had taught her to read the tracks of deer and foxes, not horses, but she could read these prints clearly enough.

The hooves had grown from the small circles which had ripped free from the rockers into massive ovals larger than Pearl's hand. Looking closely and measuring with her fingers, she decided that the horse which had taken the narrowest path, to the moor, was the largest and heaviest. It must be the chestnut stallion, Jasper's horse.

With her face so close to the path, she could see that the faint bootprints were on top of the hoofprints. The feet were larger than hers, but smaller than a man's. The prints were narrow, with a distinct heel, like riding boots.

So the boy with the stick had prevented her following the triplets, then followed them himself. And when they split up, he had chosen the same path as the largest horse.

"What I'm hunting, I won't shoot, unless I have to," he had told her.

Was he hunting Jasper, Ruby and Emerald? What possible reason could he have to *shoot* them?

Pearl rubbed at her eyes with shaky fingers. She had to decide fast: should she follow the boy following Jasper, or try to find the girls first? If she followed one of the mares, which would she choose? She couldn't tell which was Emmie's and which Ruby's from their hoofprints.

Pearl stood up, leaning forward to rest her forehead against the solid trunk of the old chestnut while she tried to decide. But her skin brushed against something soft rather than hard, so she backed away fast, and saw the dangling body of a shrew, nailed by its tail to the bark.

She was scrubbing at her forehead with the back of her hand when she heard a noise: a sob, cut off short and sudden by a dark silence.

Ruby!

Ruby had never grown out of the habit of crying prettily to get what she wanted. Or, if she didn't get everything she wanted, weeping and howling until she nearly dissolved away.

Pearl decided who to follow. Not a possible Emerald, nor a possible Jasper, but a definite Ruby. A little sister in tears, deep in the wood, who needed a big sister to comfort her, and who might be able to tell that big sister what was going on.

Pearl ran down the path into the heart of the wood, as softly and quietly as possible. It wasn't like Ruby to break off a good weep, and Pearl would prefer to see what had silenced her sister before it saw or heard her.

The path crossed a couple of clearings, areas kept free of trees and bushes to allow the lazy pheasants to enjoy the sun. Pearl realised she hadn't seen any pheasants in this pheasant wood. Maybe they had been startled recently.

Under the constant rustle of twigs and leaves, she heard the hiss of fast water over stones. Through the trees to her left, she saw a burn, rushing down from the mountains.

Then the hoofprints vanished completely under her running feet. Pearl slowed and looked behind her. The prints had veered onto the confused ground under the trees.

The horse had stepped off the path and headed for the water. Did rocking horses get thirsty?

Pearl hid behind the trunk of a wide beech tree and looked down at the banks of the burn. There were no prints, no horse and no weeping child.

She peered further upstream. There! At the edge of the water, she saw the curve of a hoofprint.

Keeping well back from the exposed bank, she crept upstream.

After five minutes of pushing through tangled scratchy bushes, she reached another clearing, where the stream spread out into a broad shallow pool. Pearl pulled back quickly into the cover of a holly bush.

On the other side of the pool stood a horse. A large horse with a pale blonde mane and tail and a peachy orange body, wearing a leather saddle, bridle and reins.

However, this horse didn't shine with grooming and good food, but with varnish. This horse, taller than Pearl, and shifting its golden hooves restlessly, was made of gleaming carved wood.

This was Ruby's palomino pony, her wooden rocking horse, now large enough to carry a man, and moving like a real muscle and bone horse.

Pearl had almost accepted that she was following the hoofmarks of galloping rocking horses. But now she had found this impossible wooden beast, her muscles clenched in disgust at whatever twisting of nature and logic had forced it into being.

The mare had her head down, gazing at her reflection in the water, swinging her elegant nose from one side to the other so she could see her eyes and nostrils and mane. She snorted with delight at her beauty.

Pearl looked round. There was no sign of Ruby. Had the horse thrown her? Had she run off?

Then she heard a familiar noise, a tiny muffled sob.

Pearl and the horse both jerked their heads up.

Ruby was perched on the lowest branch of a grey beech tree on the edge of the clearing.

The mare lunged at the child, rearing up to her full height and snapping at Ruby's boots. Ruby gasped and pulled her feet higher. The long teeth of the horse missed her by the width of a girth-strap.

Ruby was silent again, though Pearl could see tears running down her cheeks. The horse went back to gazing at herself.

Pearl looked at Ruby, clinging to the high branch. How had she got up there? Beech trees were very hard to climb: their trunks wide and smooth, their lowest branches above head height. Even standing on the horse's back, Ruby would have struggled to reach that bottom branch.

Had she actually flown? Was Pearl's unspoken suspicion actually true?

Perhaps this time, with Ruby on her own, Pearl would get a clearer answer than "I was just playing" or "It just happened", which were the triplets' usual answers to her questions about how they ended up on top of chimneys or Christmas trees.

To ask Ruby any questions, Pearl would have to get her down from the tree, and she couldn't do that until the horse was under control.

Pearl studied the horse. She was a gorgeous beast, with an arched neck and muscled haunches. But she was nervous, her eyes white-rimmed, her ears straight back and her hooves constantly moving over the ground. If she was attacking Ruby, her own rider, she certainly wouldn't allow Pearl to get close enough to soothe her and tie her up.

The mare seemed content to let Ruby stay in the tree so long as she was silent. Was the rocking horse guarding her, keeping her here for someone? Pearl had to rescue her sister before that someone arrived.

Chapter 4

Pearl watched the rocking horse's head bend lower towards the pool, as if the mare wanted to touch her own reflection. Her smooth muzzle brushed the cold water and she leapt back, surprised.

Pearl nearly giggled. Silly vain beast! What that horse really needed was a mirror!

A mirror? Pearl raised her eyebrows and started patting her many pinafore pockets. She had experimented a few weeks ago with reflections and light: setting fire to dry grass with a magnifying glass, signalling in code using reflected sunlight. Did she still have ...?

Yes! A mirror, wrapped in oilcloth, tangled up with string and stones in a right-hand pocket. It wasn't large, but at least it wasn't cracked. Pearl rubbed it with her sleeve, and looked at the horse again.

The mare was gazing at herself side on, to see her flank and legs.

Pearl took a slow breath and stepped out of the bushes. She crossed the burn in one long stride and walked round the pool towards the mare, clicking her tongue softly.

The horse wheeled round and bared her teeth.

Pearl spoke calmly, "Here girl, here girl," and

held out the mirror. She moved it slowly, so the horse could see her reflection slide across it.

Ruby called, "Pearl! Help me!"

Pearl said in the same calm voice, "Shhh. Don't distract her."

The mare stood still, staring at the mirror as Pearl approached.

"Look, aren't you pretty?" Pearl held the mirror steady so it reflected the mare's face.

She stepped nearer. The mare backed away and bared her teeth again.

Pearl looked at the restless hooves, sharp as saw blades and heavy as axes. But the horse was still staring at the mirror.

Pearl didn't want the mare near the pool; she needed her near the trees. She took a few steps to her left, towards a rowan tree, still angling the mirror at the horse.

"Look, this won't get you wet. You can touch your reflection in this." She laid the mirror on the ground under the tree and stepped back. The mare walked cautiously over, looking down, turning her head, dipping her nose down to nuzzle herself.

Pearl darted forward, grabbed the reins, yanked them over the mare's lowered head and knotted them round the sturdy trunk of the rowan tree.

Then Pearl leapt out of range as the mare suddenly realised what had happened and lashed out with her hooves, rearing and bucking. The horse didn't hit Pearl, she didn't break her jewelled bridle, she didn't splinter the tree, but as her front hooves crashed down, she did smash the mirror.

The rocking horse screamed her anger.

Pearl ran to the base of Ruby's tree. "Jump!"

"I can't."

"You have to! She'll soon snap the bridle, or pull up the tree. You have to jump NOW!"

"I can't. I'm scared!"

"I'm scared too, but I'm not sitting weeping. Jump and I'll catch you!"

"I'm safe here," sniffed Ruby. "She can't hurt me here."

"You're safe from your horrible horse there, Ruby, but someone else is tracking you all, and you won't be safe from him up there. He's got a gun. So get down here!"

Pearl heard the horse fighting to free herself. Ruby wriggled with indecision on the branch.

"Ruby Chayne, I'm going away and leaving you here on your own, if you aren't down when I've counted to ..."

Ruby jumped, without waiting for Pearl to count to anything, and landed on her sister in a pile of petticoats at the base of the beech.

The horse was now hauling backwards with all her strength. The tree was bending and the leather bridle was stretched taut.

Pearl looked round. Where could they go? More importantly, where couldn't the mare go?

She dragged Ruby round the beech tree to a clump of bushes, thick, thorny and very low to the ground. "Crawl in there and stay quiet."

They struggled under the branches and leaves, then watched from their dark hide as the bridle finally snapped and the mare almost fell onto her rear.

She regained her footing and galloped over to the beech tree. When she saw her captive had gone, the palomino slashed the trunk with her front hooves, leaving pale wounds in the bark.

Then she stalked round the pool, stepping easily over the stream, her head swinging and her ears cocked. Pearl and Ruby held their breath. Huge polished hooves passed just in front of their clenched fists and bowed heads.

After three slow searching circuits, the mare went back to the rowan tree, her neck drooping. She picked up her tattered bridle with her teeth, turned her haunches towards the girls, then galloped towards the path.

Pearl and Ruby stayed still and silent for a few breaths. Then Pearl saw movement under the rowan tree.

She slid out, catching the back of her dress on the thorns, and crept over to the disturbed ground. A gold ring, a little bigger than the circle Pearl would make with her thumb and forefinger, was tugging itself free from the tree roots and mirror fragments. Pearl watched, not as surprised as she would have been an hour ago, as the ring rose up on its edge and started to roll away, in the same direction as the mare.

Pearl dived forward and grabbed the ring. It twirled and turned in her hand, but she held it tight.

Ruby tiptoed up to her. "What is it?"

"It's part of the mare's bridle, and I think it's trying to follow her. It might be useful."

"Why? I don't ever want to see that nasty beast again."

"It might be useful to know where she's gone." Pearl sat up, dropped the gold ring in a pinafore pocket and buttoned it up tight. She felt the ring twist and bump against her leg.

"Now," she turned to her little sister, "tell me what's going on."

Ruby flopped onto the grass beside her sister and started to sob again.

Pearl found a stained hanky in another pocket and shoved it at her sister. "Stop snivelling and talk to me. Those horses still have Emmie and Jasper, so I need to know what's happening."

"But I don't know myself!" Ruby flung her arms round her big sister.

Pearl gave her a hug, then pushed her away. "Tell me what you do know."

Ruby sobbed and shook her head.

Pearl watched impatiently as her sister wept. Even with watery eyes and a dripping nose, Ruby was a very pretty child. Big green eyes, long dark lashes, slim curved eyebrows and a pouting mouth, framed by blonde curls tied with a red ribbon.

When Pearl left her hair loose, it looked like a tangle of socks. When Ruby left her hair loose, it curved and twined like vines on a statue.

Pearl gave her sister's golden curls a swift tug to get her attention and demanded again, "Tell me what you know."

Ruby gabbled, to get the telling over quickly. "We were riding our horses this morning, being knights at a tournament, when suddenly there were splintering sounds and lots of light and the window swung open. Jasper's horse jumped out first, then Emmie's, then mine and it was like flying, then the horses galloped away so fast we were whooping and laughing. Then they started to get bigger and we realised they didn't pay any attention to our feet or knees or reins and just went their own way and we couldn't stop them or slow them or turn them, so we got scared, at least I did, but then we were out through the gate and into the wood. And before we knew what was happening, the horses all took different paths and I shouted 'help' but the others didn't answer me. And my horse ran by the stream and found this pool, and I thought she was just stopping for a drink, so I slid down, and she bit my dress and I pulled away — look!" Her red dress was ripped at the shoulder. "And I thought about climbing up that tree, so I just jumped and grabbed the branch, and I was higher than I thought I could be, and I tried to think about jumping even higher, but I was too scared, so I just sat there. If I was quiet, she left me alone. And then you came." She hugged her big sister again.

Pearl said carefully, "So you didn't climb that tree. You just jumped?"

"Yes. Like the time you got me and Jasper down from the chandelier and the … em … the other times … It was just a thought and I got light and floaty for a minute and I aimed for the branch."

"Can you do it again?"

Pearl watched closely as Ruby stood and reached upwards. "No. I think my snottery nose is weighing me down." She blew noisily into Pearl's hanky and sat beside her again.

Pearl didn't demand more answers about flying. There were other vital questions. "When the rocking horses came off their rockers and leapt out of the window, was anyone else there? Did you see or hear anything else?"

"No."

"Nothing at all? No songs or words, no people or animals?"

"There were some swans in the sky. We'd just noticed them and wondered if we should be princes enchanted into swans and wait for our sister to save us, but then the horses took us away ..."

"So there were swans. Was there a tall boy? At the gate, or anywhere else?"

"No, I don't think so. Can we go home now?" Ruby rested her head on Pearl's arm.

"Home? But we have to find Emmie and Jasper."

"They can look after themselves, Pearl. Or you could come back and find them once you've taken me home."

Pearl felt the shivering ring in her pocket as she stood up. "No, we're going to find them now. Come on!"

Ruby wailed, "I don't want to see those horses again! I just want to go home to Mother. It must be nearly time for elevenses by now!"

Pearl thought of her simple mission to bring the triplets down for breakfast. "It's not nearly time for elevenses yet, Ruby, because we're not going home without the others."

Chapter 5

Pearl dragged Ruby along the path. As they walked briskly beside the mare's hoofprints, the frantic ring in Pearl's pocket calmed down, turning gently in the direction of their steps towards the chestnut tree.

Just as Pearl caught sight of the glossy green chestnut ahead, the sky above the treetops dimmed, and they heard a sudden tapping. Ruby jumped and looked round nervously.

"Calm down!" snapped Pearl. "It's only rain on the leaves!" Then she looked at the path. The few drops getting through the leaf canopy were already splattering dark dots over the hoofprints.

"Run!" she yelled. "Run! We have to follow the trail as far as we can before we lose it!"

Pearl broke into a sprint, and as soon as she reached the crossroads, she fell to her knees and tried to read the tracks. The narrow moor path, the wider river path and the straight path home, all still showed the marks of hooves. But the rain had already blurred the prints so much she couldn't tell which path now had an extra set of hoofprints. She had lost the riderless palomino's trail already.

"Hurry up!" she shouted at Ruby, who was

running into the raindrops in a flappy, half-hearted way.

"I can't. My legs are sore."

By the time Ruby had panted up to the tree, the paths had darkened almost to black, and the prints were nearly gone.

"What do you think, Ruby, should we head for the moors or the river? Should we follow Jasper or Emmie?" But her little sister was shivering too much to answer.

"You are pathetic, Ruby! If you ran faster you'd keep yourself warm!"

Ruby's bottom lip quivered.

"Oh, for goodness sake!" Pearl would never catch up with the other two if she had to keep mollycoddling Ruby. She hauled her sister off the path into a stand of birch trees, where she had spotted a line so straight it must be man-made.

"Where are we going now?" Ruby whimpered, as Pearl felt the ring jump violently in her pocket.

"I'm going to find you shelter, and you're going to stay there until I get back."

"But I want to go *home!*"

"If you can go home all on your own, and not meet any wooden horses or boys with guns, then fine, off you go. Or you can wait here, and I'll come back for you."

In front of them was a wooden hut, which Pearl guessed was the gamekeepers' storeroom.

Pearl pushed the door, but it was locked. She knelt down and looked at the keyhole. A hand's width below it, a hole was drilled in the wood. She carefully poked two fingers in, and felt a rough string dangling behind the door. Pearl nodded. The gardener's toolshed at home used the same trick.

She gripped the string between her fingers, and pulled it through. There was a key tied to the end. She unlocked the door and waved Ruby in.

Ruby wrinkled her nose at the stink of aniseed, a smell pheasants love so much the keepers used it to encourage them to stay in the wood. Ruby tried to back out again, but Pearl gave her a gentle shove. "At least it's dry," Pearl said firmly, as she found a stool, a blanket and a tin of shortbread among the full bags of grain and empty chick coops. "These will keep you warm and fed. So stay here, and stay quiet."

Ruby gulped down a sob.

"I'll lock the door when I leave," Pearl said, "then I'll push the key back through. Untie the key and keep it in your pocket so no one else can get in. Don't unlock the door until I get back. Don't unlock it for *anyone else*. No one else but me."

"How will I know it's you? Should we have a password?"

"A password?" Pearl laughed. "Passwords are for people who don't know each other, like spies. If you don't recognise my voice, I'll just tell you what I think of your new beaded frock. No one else in the whole world will be as honest as me."

Pearl gave Ruby a quick kiss and left, locking the door and shoving the key back through.

She was on her own again, but at least she could move faster now.

She ran back to the chestnut tree, where the horses had split up, and where the shrew still dangled. The rain had wiped away all the hoofprints. There were no tracks left to follow.

Pearl thought for a moment, then unbuttoned her pocket and grasped the twisting ring between wet fingers.

"You want to be reunited with your horse and her bridle, don't you? I can't follow Emmie or Jasper, but if I follow Ruby's horse I might find out what's going on."

She flicked the golden ring into the air, and watched it fall to the ground faster than the silver raindrops.

The instant the hoop hit the path, it began to roll.

It moved faster than Pearl expected; she had to run to keep up as it sped along the path towards the moor. She hoped it was leading her to Ruby's mare and Jasper's stallion. She hoped she wasn't following the boy with the burnt black stick.

The rain was slowing to a drizzle, almost as if it had done its work obscuring the trail, and as the last drops fell to the ground, Pearl burst out of the woods into the deer forest.

The name always made her smile. It had been one of Emmie's favourite jokes when she was little: what kind of forest has no trees? A deer forest.

A deer forest was land where deer were bred, stalked and hunted. In Scotland, that was rarely woodland; it was usually moorland and mountaintops.

So Pearl followed the golden circle out of the trees into the treeless forest.

The hoop stopped, balanced on its edge, then began to roll uphill towards the first ridge. The path was bumpy and rough, and the ring skipped and wavered. Pearl, running hard, was able to keep close behind.

Then the ring rolled straight into a stone, and ricocheted off like a billiard ball. Spinning backwards, it banged into Pearl's right boot. She stumbled and stood hard on the hoop. When she lifted her foot, the ring lay flat and still on the path, crushed into the ground.

"Sorry!" she said automatically. She shook her head at her own clumsiness and at her attempt to apologise to a bit of metal. Then she tried again. "Come on. Get up. We need to find that horse."

She bent forward, and stroked the motionless hoop with her fingers. Suddenly it sprang up, hitting her hard on the nose, and rolled off.

Pearl followed, rubbing her nose and staying further back this time.

The ring led her to the top of the ridge, and a perfect view of land she only knew from her brother's maps.

The top drawer of Pearl's desk was packed full of Peter's maps, locked securely against Mother's panicked clearouts: maps her older brother had drawn when he was younger than the triplets, of the garden and the road to Perth; maps he had drawn when he was Pearl's age, of the pathless moorland ahead and the rocky mountains above, with tiny notes of campsites and caves and other intriguing places; maps he had drawn when he was older, of climbing holidays in the Cuillins and the Alps.

And his final map. A map of the trench in France where he spent his last days. A map with depth rather than height. A pencil sketch of a long muddy hole.

Pearl didn't need to carry these maps in her pockets; she held all the details in her head.

As she followed the ring off the ridge, she could see to the southeast the rocks marked on Peter's maps as the Twa Corbies, and further off, the River Stane curving south round the base of the mountains.

It looked as if nothing large could possibly hide in the open moor. There were no trees or hills to shelter behind. Surely a huge wooden horse, or a missing younger brother, could be seen at a glance.

But Pearl knew, from long frustrating days stalking on similar ground to the north, that an antlered stag and a dozen hinds could hide from hunters just a few yards away.

The moor ahead was crumpled, like a rug shoved up against a wall. Dozens of streams from the mountains had worn away narrow gullies. There were soft soggy bogs in sudden hollows, and tangles of low ridges which made it hard to walk in a straight line.

Ruby's horse, Jasper's horse, Jasper, the boy with the stick, even Emmie and her horse, they could all be in the deer forest ahead of her, and Pearl wouldn't find them unless she fell right over them.

Or followed this spinning golden ring.

The ring had been moving more slowly through the maze of heather stalks. Then suddenly it rolled faster again, over a patch of grass at the bottom of a slope. Pearl spotted a hoofprint where the heather met the grass, so she knew they were on the right track.

The ring skipped merrily over the bright green ground, quivering on the surface like a skimming stone, then it wobbled and started to sink.

Pearl jerked backwards. She suddenly realised why the ground was soft enough to hold a print even after rain.

This slope slid downhill into a bog.

"No! Come back!" But it was too late. The ring couldn't roll back or forward in the soft wet ground. It was being slowly sucked down.

From a tuft of dry heather, Pearl watched the ring founder. It twisted and twitched, but couldn't free itself. More than half its edge had sunk into the grasping earth. Its movements were getting smaller and more feeble.

Pearl knew the best advice for people trapped in bogs was: 'Don't struggle! Struggling makes you sink in further. Stay still and shout for help.'

The only person who could answer the ring's silent call for help was Pearl. But if she got stuck, if she shouted for help, who would answer her call? She didn't want to summon a rocking horse, or the tall boy.

Pearl hesitated. If she tried to rescue the ring, she could be caught in the bog herself. But if she didn't, she would lose her last chance of following the rocking horses and of finding Jasper and Emmie.

The ring, heavy with mud, had stopped moving.

Pearl searched the ground for anything she could use as a hook.

There were no trees in the deer forest, so there were no branches lying around. Heather stems and roots were too bent and knotted to reach any distance.

The only available tools were her own arms and hands. Pearl groaned in frustration. The ring was almost gone. She had to decide before it vanished completely. Would she risk herself for her brother and sister?

Of course she would.

So Pearl took off her pinafore and lay down at the edge of the bog. She spread her weight as widely as she could and inched forward towards the ring.

She reached out her right hand. The ring was barely visible now, and there were bubbles popping round it as it sank. She couldn't quite touch it.

She flexed her toes against the springy heather and forced herself forward, feeling cold dampness seeping into her dress. As she pushed yet again, her body sank slightly into the clammy ground.

She stretched her arm. Her nails clicked on the metal. She risked one more push with her toes, and felt the ring with her fingertips. She eased it out of the mud and clutched it tight.

She wanted to leap up and run for the heather, but she knew that could be fatal, so she slid slowly backwards.

Her feet and legs were safe on the heather. Then her hips and waist.

She tried to drag her shoulders and torso through the bog, which made terrifying slurping sounds as it held her in its grip.

Pearl couldn't bear the feel of the ground holding her down, so she jerked up and swivelled round, shoving herself up onto the heather with her left hand. That hand and wrist were sucked down, but the rest of her was free. She leant backwards, using her whole weight to pull her hand out with a belch of boggy air. She fell over and stared at the sky. The ring wriggled between her fingers.

The daft hoop was still trying to roll right over the misleading green grass to where the long-legged mare had landed safely on the other side. If Pearl let it go now, it would just dive into the bog again.

She held the ring tightly as she rubbed her hands clean on the heather, and covered the worst of the dirt on her dress with her pinafore.

Then she walked round the edge of the bog, and let the ring go at the other side.

The hoop bounced carelessly over the heather as if it had been in no danger at all. It clattered down a steep gully, right through a burn, and back up the other side. The dip in the water washed it bright gold again, so Pearl could see it easily. It was rushing towards the Twa Corbies.

Pearl didn't think the mossy grey boulders were big enough to hide people and horses. Then she remembered a gully marked on Peter's maps, running along the side of the eastern Corbie, cut into the ground by a wide mountain stream. There might be enough shelter in there for a whole herd of rocking horses.

She decided to let the ring go on ahead and follow at a careful distance. She didn't want to meet Ruby's palomino again without warning. She lowered herself into the thick heather, where she was surrounded by the warm scents of honey, thyme and juniper, and sudden rank whiffs of fox and weasel.

She watched the ring curve round the Twa Corbies and leap into the gully beyond. Now she had lost sight of it, perhaps forever.

Pearl followed cautiously, not pressing her weight widely as she had on the bog, but moving lightly on hands and elbows, knees and toes.

What would she see when she reached the edge?

If the gully was empty, and the ring had spun out of sight, her caution would have cost Pearl her last link to the triplets and the horses that had taken them.

Pearl tried not to hear the blood beating in her ears, and the dry rustling of the heather. She listened to the sounds in the empty space beyond the rocks. And she heard laughter.

Chapter 6

It was Jasper's laugh. Ringing, chiming, tinkling.
Pearl thought he must be trying hard to make
someone like him.

She edged round the Twa Corbies, trying to
creep as slowly as the glaciers she knew had
formed this landscape. Her face was so close to the
heather it pricked her eyeballs as she peered over
the top of the gully.

She grinned. The hunter had found her quarry.
Two horses, and two boys.

The chestnut stallion stood proudly over Jasper,
horsehair tail swishing behind his glossy wooden
rump.

The palomino mare stood beside the boy from
the gateway, her ripped bridle draped round her
drooping head and twitching ears.

The tall boy was resting on a large rock, with
his legs stretched out. His gun and stick lay by his
right hand and he was twisting the golden bridle
ring in his left hand while he talked to Jasper, who
was sitting by the older boy's feet, gazing up at
him.

Jasper's big green eyes were fixed on the tall
boy's face, and his mouth was partly open, his
lips stained purple with blaeberry juice. At every

dramatic pause in the story, Jasper nodded, giggled or asked an encouraging question.

Pearl wasn't near enough to hear the boys' words. This gully twisted and turned as the water found the best way down from the mountain. If she crept round a bend she might get nearer to the boys without being noticed, then she could hear what was going on.

Pearl retreated past the rocks, moved up the edge of the gully just out of sight of the boys and horses, and approached them again from behind. Now she couldn't see them, but she could hear better.

"So, if you bring me your sisters, I will bring you your destiny."

Pearl recognised the tall boy's voice, though now it sounded inspiring rather than mocking.

"Why do you need them?" asked Jasper. "You have me. They're just girls. Ruby cries and Emmie asks awkward questions."

"We need them because the three of you are the jewels which will crown my grandfather Lord of the Mountains."

"Once we find the girls, once we've crowned your grandfather, what happens then?"

Pearl nodded. Jasper had asked the question she would have asked.

"Then you'll have the honour of helping our family hold the power of the mountains as well as the moors."

"Why do you need us for that? Can't you just buy the mountains?"

"It's not about money and legal papers, Jasper.

It's about taking responsibility for the land, listening to its music, using the lore to store and share its power."

Pearl was as close as she could get, so she heard the tall boy's unlikely words perfectly.

"No one has sung with the mountains since the Grey Men died, so they're suffering from neglect. But we can't sing with them until the war ends."

"The war?" Jasper sounded shocked. "But the war ended in 1918!"

"Not the Great War, Jasper. We don't need a peace treaty to end this war; we just need to crown my grandfather. So let's go and search for your sisters."

Pearl, lying as still and low as a stone in the heather, frowned. If the boys left the gully on horseback, how could she keep up with them?

"But where will we find them?" Jasper objected. "I haven't seen the girls since my stallion brought me here. Ruby's mare must have followed us, but I don't know where Ruby is. I was going to look for her after I'd had a snack, honestly I was. But then you appeared. How did you find me?"

"I knew your stallion had galloped onto the moor, but I didn't know where you were hiding. Then I heard the mare's hooves and saw her leap down here. She's found her brother, now we have to find your sisters."

"But how?"

"Well, we know someone separated Ruby from her horse ..."

Pearl held her breath guiltily for a moment. But the boy couldn't know she had tricked the horse, nor that she was just above him.

He kept talking, "… and the tracks of Emerald's horse led round the mountains towards the Laird of Swanhaugh's lands. It's the Laird who's fighting us for the right to the mountains, so he might have forced the horses to split up, like he sometimes forces the land to do his will. He might even have captured your sisters. He's a vicious man, but he probably won't hurt them while there's a chance he can use them to crown himself."

Pearl frowned. Perhaps she was going to meet all her strange neighbours today. The Laird of Swanhaugh was an eccentric who never ventured out of his parklands to local events. Her mother didn't disapprove of him, but the local gossips did.

Jasper was still asking questions. "How will you make him give Emmie and Ruby back? Can he do magic like you?"

The tall boy laughed. "I don't do magic, Jasper, I just hear the music of the land. But the Laird is also skilled in landlore, and he won't give up the girls easily. However, we have a few advantages. He's ready to defend himself against my grandfather, but he's never duelled with me. He's tired of the long war, but I'm fresh."

Pearl considered what she was hearing. Were there any useful facts in the boy's wild fairy tale? He was involved in a disagreement over land, and thought the triplets could help him, when really he'd be better off with a decent lawyer. He was trying to persuade Jasper to join him with dangerous words like "destiny". But he'd lost the girls, and thought they were both with the Laird.

Pearl knew Ruby was safe in the keepers' shed, but what if Emmie was with the boy's enemy?

Pearl had discovered Ruby guarded by a violent horse and Jasper being entranced by a dangerous boy. She wondered who she'd have to defeat to free Emmie.

She shook her head. She couldn't get distracted by unanswerable questions or vague fears; she had to concentrate on saving her family one by one.

There was no point in grabbing Jasper and trying to run home. Even on the bumpy moorland, the horses would overtake them. She would have to distract the boy, sneak Jasper away and hide him until it was safe to go home.

The boy was still talking, his voice warm and persuasive.

"Your names are part of your destiny. Jasper, Emerald and Ruby, three precious gems."

Where could she hide Jasper? After a searching look round the deer forest, she stared at the Twa Corbies. Which symbol had her brother drawn beside them on his maps? She hoped she remembered correctly.

Her fingers poked around under the heather until she found a couple of pebbles. The boy's voice rolled round the gully as she weighed them in her hand.

"The horses were a gift from us, to protect you until you were old enough for the crowning ceremony. They did their job today, getting you away from the Laird's ambush. I just wish they hadn't split up! If they'd stayed together I would have all three of you already."

Pearl lifted her arm and flung one stone as hard as she could over the top of the gully to the other side.

It landed silently in the heather. She sighed.

She lifted her arm again and flung the other stone. It clattered on a rock.

The boy below stopped talking. Pearl held her breath until she saw him clambering up the other side of the gully, towards the noise.

Pearl slid her head and shoulders over the edge. "Oi!" she whispered to Jasper. "Come up here now!"

Jasper looked at her and frowned. She mouthed, "NOW!" and reached her arm down to him.

He shrugged and climbed towards her.

She grabbed him, almost lifting him off his feet, though he was nearly as tall as her, then she ran with him towards the rocks.

Behind them, the horses neighed in alarm. But however swift rocking horses were on the flat, they wouldn't be very fast scrambling up the gully's steep sides.

Pearl and Jasper sprinted to the Twa Corbies, where she shoved her brother through a tiny gap she'd guessed was hidden between the two grey rocks, into the cramped cave which Peter had marked on his maps.

As she got used to the dim light, she noticed words scratched into the rock at the narrow entrance. *Peter Chayne, August 1915.* Her big brother had been here exactly twelve years ago. She ran her fingers over the grooves forming his name.

Jasper wriggled beside her, jabbing his elbow into her leg.

"Be quiet, and they might not find us," she whispered.

"What are you doing, dragging me in here?" he whispered back.

"Saving you from that boy and his horrid horses."

"That boy is my friend and my stallion is fantastic. I don't *want* saved!" Jasper's voice was rising.

"Shhhh!" Pearl slapped her hand over his mouth. He squirmed.

"Shh shh shh, Jasper," she murmured, like he was a wee boy again. "Shhhh."

He bit her fingers and shoved her off.

Then he screamed, "I'm here! I'm here!" His voice rattled round the tiny space.

"You little ... toad!" spat Pearl. "I don't know why I bother ..."

"Come out, dearest Jasper." The tall boy's voice moved nearer as he spoke. "Come on out."

Jasper pushed past Pearl and slid out.

She crouched on the cold ground. Would her brother betray her, or would he leave her, hidden and safe?

She didn't really have to wonder.

"I didn't run off, really I didn't. She grabbed me. I bit her, though, and that's when I shouted. She's still in there. "

"What a hero you are, Jasper. Shall we ask her to come out too?"

Pearl pressed herself to the back of the stone space.

A voice whispered just outside, "Will you come out? Or shall I come in and get you?"

Pearl shivered, and looked at the narrow entrance. She remembered the boy as tall but slim, and he could probably fit through. She would rather meet him again, if she had to, in a larger space than this.

"I'm coming out."

She squeezed out awkwardly, to the cool smile of the tall boy and the sideways smirk of her revolting little brother.

"A brave rescue attempt," sneered the boy. "It might even have succeeded, except Jasper didn't want to be rescued. Just a slight flaw in your plan."

Pearl glared at Jasper as she stood up. He retreated, muttering, "This is my big sister."

"We've met," said the boy, towering over both of them. "I thought I'd left you safely at home. You must be brighter than you look." He glanced in amusement at her muddy clothes.

Then he looked behind him very briefly, perhaps checking the horses were out of sight. He began to twirl his stick.

"Your brother and I were just exploring the deer forest. I'll look after him, so you can go home now, you don't need to worry."

"Of course I need to worry. You're filling his head with nonsense about wars and destiny. We've had enough of that in our family. It's not Jasper's destiny to fight anyone else's war. There's no such thing as destiny. He can make his own decisions."

The tall boy was now staring at Pearl. Not at her

dirty hands, or lumpy pinafore, but at her eyes. His stick swung faster.

"What did you hear me say?" he asked sharply. "Before you tried to run off with Jasper, what did you hear?"

Pearl shrugged. "I hardly heard anything. I couldn't get much closer than this."

"But you heard us talk about the war and Jasper's destiny. What else did you hear?"

Though she hadn't understood or believed most of what he'd said in the gully, it didn't seem sensible to admit she'd heard his silly secrets. So instead she turned to Jasper.

"Come on, let's leave this boy and his daft wargames. Mother's probably got elevenses ready now, so come home, and we'll find Emmie and Ruby later."

Jasper glanced at the tall boy, who smiled. "So, Jasper, do you want to go home with your big sister for tea and toast, or do you want to come with me and fulfil your destiny?"

Pearl's brother hesitated, then took a deliberate step towards the tall boy, who immediately slowed the moving stick so it didn't hit Jasper.

The moment the stick stopped creating its pattern, Pearl heard the crashing and scrambling of hooves. The palomino leapt over the edge of the gully and galloped straight at her, with teeth bared, ears flat back and white-rimmed eyes looking for revenge.

Chapter 7

The huge rocking horse hurtled towards Pearl, heavy wooden hooves hammering on the ground.

Pearl forced herself to stand still. There was no point in running away. She waited until the horse was nearly on top of her, then flung herself to the right, as the massive hooves rushed past her.

She jumped up as the mare skidded to a halt on the heather and swerved back round.

Pearl was trembling. Would the horse charge again? Could she clamber up the Twa Corbies before the horse reached her?

Suddenly the tall boy stepped forward. He stood between Pearl and the horse, his back to Pearl, his left hand out towards the mare. "Whoa, girl. Calm down, calm down. Leave her alone. I'll deal with her. Whoa, my beauty, whoa."

The mare obeyed. Her hooves didn't move, but she was still breathing hard, her wooden ribcage creaking. The boy kept speaking soothingly until her eyes lost their white rims, until her ears moved forward again.

Pearl had time to slow her own breathing before he turned back to her. "My horse doesn't like you. I wonder why?"

"I've no idea," lied Pearl, ignoring the tattered

bridle on the horse's neck.

"So you've not seen this horse before?"

It was tempting to say, "Of course, lots of times, in the schoolroom." But she didn't want this boy to realise how much she suspected, so Pearl simply said, "No."

"And you don't know where either of your sisters are?"

"No."

"We need to talk. Jasper, lead your sister down to your blaeberries and your stallion, while I coax the mare back down."

Jasper slithered down the gully to the stones by the burn. Pearl zigzagged after him.

When they reached the bottom, Jasper asked angrily, "Why are you interfering? I'm having an adventure all of my own and I don't need you."

"I don't think you're safe with that boy. I don't like these impossible horses and I don't trust his talk about destiny. People told our big brother it was his destiny to defend his country, and look what happened to him."

"That won't happen to me." Jasper jumped onto a rock. "I'm special. He says so. I will be very important and very powerful. That is my destiny."

"Jasper, you fool, there's no such thing as destiny. He's just trying to persuade you to do something you'd refuse to do if it wasn't dressed up in fancy words. We have to get you out of here. Do exactly as I say, and we'll be home soon."

Pearl looked at the birch trees growing by the water. They were short but sturdy. She tugged at a thin white branch, trying to think of a plan to defeat two wooden horses, an older boy and a petulant little brother.

Jasper stamped his foot. "I'm not going to do what you say!" His purple-stained mouth opened wide as he shrieked louder. "I'm going to be a power in the land, and you won't get to boss me around any more!"

The tall boy and the mare appeared at the top of the gully. The boy strode down the slope towards Pearl, speaking right over the top of Jasper. His voice wasn't inspiring, or sneering, or amused. It was angry and hard. "I found the flattened heather where you lay, like a sneak, eavesdropping. From there I could hear every word you were saying down here, even before your delightful little brother started having a tantrum.

"You heard *everything* I said, didn't you?"

He stopped very close to Pearl, the two horses either side of him. She could smell the walnut oil from their shiny flanks.

Pearl didn't like lying on principle, and she wasn't very good at it anyway. So she shrugged. "I did hear some of what you said. But I didn't understand it."

"You heard about the mountains? The jewels? The landlore?"

She nodded. "You may have convinced Jasper with your fairy tales, but you didn't convince me."

"I didn't convince you?" He scowled. "But you still heard me!

"Guard her," he ordered the horses, then stomped away and kicked out viciously at a stone. It splashed into the burn, getting his perfect boots wet. The drops glistened for a moment on the leather, then slid off.

Pearl, trying to ignore the two horses staring at her, heard him mutter, "Damn! I'm making a complete mess of this war already. I've lost two triplets and I've told our secrets to a girl who can't even hear the land! Damn, damn, damn!"

He kicked another stone, took a deep breath, then turned back to Pearl and Jasper. He spoke slowly and deliberately. "Alright. This is what we'll do. Jasper, the horses will take you to my grandfather's house, and your big sister will come with me to find the girls."

He waved the horses away from Pearl and smiled charmingly at her. "We'll work better as a team, don't you think?"

Pearl wasn't any more impressed by his charm than she had been by his sneers or his threats.

"No. Jasper will stay with me, and you can take your nasty horses home to Grandpa. I'll find my sisters myself. I can deal with the Laird."

The boy's smile dropped off his face. "You may not be convinced by me, but if you challenged the Laird he would convince you, just before he crushed you. If you want your sisters, work with me or go straight home."

He twisted his fingers swiftly, and the two rocking horses crowded even closer to Pearl. The sun was shining behind the mare and the stallion, casting stark shadows and harsh lines on their carved skulls. The exaggerated sweep of their eyebrows hid their eyes. Their wooden ears pointed straight at Pearl, as sharp as arrowheads.

"I'm not scared of them, I'm not scared of the Laird, and I'm not scared of you." She clenched her fists, so her fingers wouldn't tremble as the cold golden mare came nearer.

The boy laughed. "You aren't scared? Really?"

He flicked his fingers and the horses moved back again. Pearl's hands uncurled a little.

"Sit down." He waved grandly at the chair-sized rocks. "Sit down. I think we need each other. We shouldn't fight."

Pearl remained standing. "Why do we need each other?"

"I know how to defeat the Laird, and you know where … you know the girls. They trust you. As you've just discovered, it's hard to rescue someone who doesn't want to be rescued." He glanced over at Jasper, sitting on a rock, gobbling blaeberries again. "Perhaps you should have hit him on the head before you hid him?"

Pearl tried not to smile. She had wondered the same herself.

The boy continued his argument in a gentle voice. "When I find the girls with the Laird, they may not know which of us to trust, particularly if he's charmed them rather than scared them. But if you're with me, they'll trust me. Then I can rescue them."

But Pearl wasn't persuaded by a shared joke and a soft voice. "There's a slight flaw in your rescue plan too, I'm afraid."

"Really? What flaw?"

She raised her eyebrows. "I don't trust you myself, and I don't believe your story. Even if I did,

I don't think it's my sisters' duty to help you in some petty feud with your neighbours."

He wheeled away from her, and his voice hardened. "You heard what I said to Jasper, but you weren't really listening, were you? Typical! You people stomp all over the surface of the land, but you don't ever listen to it."

Pearl's voice rose in anger to match his. "Are you telling me I don't listen to the world around me? Are you telling me I can't read the land? I tracked two horses here faster than you did." She jabbed her finger in turn at each of them, her quarry successfully tracked and taken. "I found you, I crept up on you, I listened to your secrets and I stole Jasper from you with a trick a three-year-old wouldn't have fallen for. I can read and hunt the land better than anyone else here."

The boy strode round her, flinging words at her. "You can read it, but you can't hear its music or feel its pain! You might notice the thin grass, skinny game and flaking stones in the mountains, but you don't know that the bedrock underneath is turning cold and brittle. And you can't do anything to help or heal the land." He paused, breathless with passion.

Pearl frowned. Before she could ask the dozen questions his words had prompted, he spoke again, more quietly. "If we don't sing with the land, it loses its music, then its strength. The Horsburghs and Swanns have fought over these mountains, rather than cared for them, for too long. We've even lost the key which lets us sing to them. If the war doesn't end soon, there will be no mountains left to fight over. That's why we need to defeat the Laird; that's why we need the triplets."

Pearl waited. He seemed to have run out of words. So she asked the most important question. "Why the triplets?"

"Because they can hear the music of the land too."

Chapter 8

The tall boy called, "You can hear the land, can't you, Jasper?"

"Can't I what?" Jasper looked up.

"Shh, just listen." He walked over and put his hand on Jasper's shoulder.

Pearl could hear the water shooshing, the birch trees creaking, the horses' hooves shifting, the boys' breaths whistling. She heard a stag boom in the tops, and the machine-gun call of a startled grouse on the moor.

She watched Jasper and the boy. Their faces were still, their eyes half shut.

The boy whispered, "Now sing back, Jasper."

Jasper started to hum a tune which swirled round and round, moving like the water at their feet, the air around them. The older boy smiled, a small serious smile.

Then he joined in. Pearl shook her head. The triplets always did that: sang new songs no one else had ever heard, as if they came into each of their heads at the same time.

The boy started adding consonants, vowels, syllables, almost but not quite words. Jasper's eyes snapped open. Like he recognised something. Like he understood what the boy was singing. Then he started to sing along. After a few bars, his eyes bright and his purple mouth wide, he leapt ahead, anticipating, singing new sounds and words before the boy.

Then the boy pointed his stick at the water, which swirled faster round the rocks, catching the sunlight in rainbows and sparkles. But Jasper didn't look down, he looked up and sang his own melody more insistently.

Suddenly a brace of pheasants rose from the heather by the Twa Corbies and circled above the gully. Another pheasant joined them, then two more. They were usually clumsy birds, but these pheasants twisted gracefully above Jasper's head, until the boys stopped on the same note, and the pheasants bellyflopped into the heather by the rocks.

The tall boy frowned for a moment, then patted Jasper's back. He raised his eyebrows at Pearl. "Did you hear that? Did you hear the land sing back to us?"

"She can't hear any music," jeered Jasper. "She gets lost in the middle of *Three Blind Mice*."

The boy tipped his head back and looked down his straight nose at Pearl. "Jasper sings with the land, so I'm sure his sisters can too. Even though they've never been taught landlore, the land's power is all around them. Can't you feel it?"

Pearl was silent. Of course she could feel it, everyone could. The triplets had always been special. She sat down on a rock away from the boys.

Jasper hummed a bar of the tune. "We just sing these for fun. We didn't know they were powerful.

Can you show me how to be powerful?"

"Yes, but first we have to find your sisters."

The boy turned to Pearl. "So that's why the Laird mustn't control Emerald and Ruby. That's why you have to help me get them back."

"Why will they be worse off with the Laird than with you?" Pearl snapped. "You kidnap children! You set violent wooden beasts on them."

"I didn't kidnap anyone!" Thomas said indignantly. "The horses were created to keep the triplets safe, so when they sensed danger from Swanhaugh this morning, they got the children out of your house. But the Laird may have forced at least one horse and two girls onto his own land."

"Will the Laird hurt them?" Pearl asked.

"I don't think so, they're too valuable. But he might not persuade them with stories and songs. He might threaten them."

"Threaten them? With what?"

"The Laird uses the land's power differently from us. My grandfather and I listen to the land and store its power simply to keep the land strong."

Pearl snorted. "No one has land and power, and doesn't use it for themselves."

"We don't use it like the Laird." The boy glanced up at the summits, and Pearl thought she saw fear in his eyes. "We no longer use blood to deepen the land's music, but the Laird enjoys bloodlore too much to give it up. Also, he uses his stored power to force the land to move for him. My family would never do that either, because compelling the land harms it rather than heals it.

"I think he used bloodlore to split up the horses

today, so if your sisters won't help him, he might use it to scare them. Do they scare easily?"

"Ruby does," Jasper answered, "but Emmie doesn't. Emmie isn't afraid of anything."

"Emmie is the sister on the white horse, isn't she? The one that went round the mountains. I wonder if she'll still be brave by the time we get there."

He faced Pearl with his hands open in front of him. "So, even though you can't hear the land, I've given you our secrets. Will you give me your help?"

She folded her arms. "I didn't ask for your secrets. And I won't promise you my help. However, if you show me where you think my sisters are, we can travel together until I get them back. But what do we do with Jasper?"

"Yes," said the boy. "What do we do with Jasper?"

They both looked at him.

He smiled back, covered in berry juice and confident, as always, that he'd get what he wanted if he just smiled nicely. "Can I come too? Can I ride my chestnut stallion and come with you?"

"NO!" shouted both older children in unison. They glanced at each other, and the boy grinned.

"No," repeated Pearl more gently. "I don't want you going anywhere near this Laird."

"He could stay here, guarded by the horses," suggested the boy.

"I don't think that's safe," said Pearl. "Perhaps the horses aren't as clever as you think. After all, the palomino lost Ruby."

The boy looked from Pearl to the mare and back. "Yes. I wonder how that happened."

"The horses could take Jasper back home," Pearl said casually.

"That wouldn't be safe either. There are too many swans over your land. He really must go to my grandfather."

"Where is your grandfather?"

"Horsburgh Hall, just a couple of miles over the moor. I know you never come and visit us, but you must have seen it. He'll be safe there."

"But you're trying to involve him in a war. That's not safe," insisted Pearl.

The boy sat down beside Jasper and thought for a while. Then he spoke softly to Pearl. "Let's make a deal. Let's work together to find the girls, then once we've reunited all three triplets, I'll try to persuade them their destiny lies with me and the power of the land; and I give you my word that you will have an equal chance to persuade them their destiny lies with cocoa and cakes at home. Does that sound fair?"

Pearl considered his offer. Ruby was safe in the woods, separated from her rocking horse, hidden from this tall boy and his destiny. So he wouldn't be able to get all three together anyway. And she might need his knowledge of the southern lands to find Emmie.

She looked at Jasper. Was it wise to let him go to Horsburgh Hall? Her mother had never let them meet the neighbours, but Pearl knew that their housekeepers occasionally nodded to each other in the shops in Perth. Surely Jasper would be safe for a few hours in a building filled with adults? Surely he'd be sensible enough to wait there for her?

Then she wondered, if they ever did have to argue their cases, what choice would Jasper make? "Are you hungry, Jasper?"

"Starving," he groaned.

She laughed. "A choice between destiny and cakes. That sounds fair. Once we have all three, not before. So first, we go and get Emmie. And Ruby, of course."

The boy pulled a small notebook out of his pocket and scribbled a note. He handed it to Jasper. "Give this to my grandfather, so he knows who you are and where I've gone." He glanced at Pearl. "And the housekeeper will feed you as many cakes as you can eat."

He led the horses up the side of the gully. Pearl and Jasper followed.

Pearl gave Jasper a hug. He squirmed away. "Be polite to his grandfather," she said sternly, "but don't agree to anything until I arrive. And stay there until I come to collect you. Do you hear me?"

Jasper grunted and leapt onto the stallion's back. Pearl watched as the two horses galloped west across the moorland, carrying her brother even further from home.

The tall boy turned to her and smiled. Pearl scowled at him. He held out his hand for her to shake. She ignored it.

"I should introduce myself. I'm Thomas Horsburgh, grandson of the Earl of Horsburgh. May I ask your name, Miss Chayne?"

Pearl stared at him. She'd guessed who he was when he first mentioned his grandfather, and realised her guess was right when he admitted to living at Horsburgh Hall. Thomas Horsburgh. The beloved only grandchild of the biggest landowner in the county. Local gossip said Thomas was sent off to the poshest school in England, and only came back to Scotland for short holidays, but he was still provided with the best horses and guns. The best of everything. When the women gossiped, he was a spoilt brat. When the girls giggled, he was tall, dark and handsome. But no one had said he was dangerous.

He repeated the question. "May I ask your name?"

"You may ask, but I can't be bothered telling it to someone so small and insignificant."

His eyebrows rose into his shiny black curls, then he laughed. "Was that what I said at the gate? I'm sorry, that was rude of me. I underestimated you. But we're allies now, aren't we? Maybe you aren't so small and insignificant after all."

"That shouldn't matter, though, should it?" she said quietly. "You can't just despise people until you need them."

"I'm sorry. I was worried about the triplets and I didn't want to be protecting anyone else. I was trying to annoy you, so you would go safely home. It didn't work, did it?"

"You did annoy me. But I won't go home until we find the girls."

"We will find them. Together." He held out his hand again.

"Alright. Together." She took his hand. It was warm and smooth. "My name is Pearl."

He looked at her with sudden sharp interest.

"Pearl! A gift from the water! I wonder ..."

"It's just a name. It doesn't mean anything. I'm not an ingredient in anyone's magic spell."

"All names mean something."

Pearl shook her head. "We've no time for wordgames. We have to find the Laird. Which way do we go?"

Thomas settled the gun and the stick in the crook of his arm, and pointed south. "We go through the mountains."

Chapter 9

Pearl didn't wait for Thomas to lead the way through the mountains.

She studied the range before her, matching it to her memory of Peter's maps. The most direct way through the mountains was the saddle-shaped pass cutting low between the Anvil and the Keystone Peak: the pass called the Grey Men's Grave.

Pearl marched up the edge of the gully, heading for the curved line of the pass, harsh and dark against the bright sky. She walked faster than she normally would on steep heather, determined not to let Thomas get ahead, determined to reach Emmie before him.

Her feet moved across land she had only traced with her fingers on maps before today. She knew the names, the heights and the contours of these mountains, but she had never breathed their air.

To the east, the Anvil was a massive wedge of a mountain, scarred by gullies and corries, weeping with burns and waterfalls. It cast a thick cold shadow over the whole pass.

The Keystone Peak, on the west side of the pass, was higher than the Anvil, its sharp summit soaring up into the sunlight from a long narrow ridge and a silver plateau.

Pearl saw the Keystone Peak's elegant summit every day from her bedroom window. It was only sketched on Peter's maps, with very little detail. Perhaps it was the only one in the range he hadn't climbed. Would she ever climb it herself?

Pearl wasn't afraid of the mountains' grey shadows, though she'd never climbed with so little equipment, nor without a companion she could trust. But if Father wanted to take Jasper into the mountains instead of her, she'd better get used to climbing alone.

She glanced behind her at the moor. To the north, she saw the square grey box of her home, with a pair of swans circling the roof. Over to the northwest, almost hidden in the wrinkles of the moor, she saw an older, darker house, with many more stable buildings. Horsburgh Hall.

Pearl sometimes felt Mother didn't care where her eldest daughter wandered, but now she realised Mother cared enough to warn her about the Horsburghs. And Pearl had just sent Jasper to their Hall.

She imagined the wreckage at home as Mother scrubbed and rearranged, and she strode even faster up the slope. She had to get all three triplets home soon.

Pearl moved like a gamekeeper or a shepherd, in long smooth strides. No effort wasted, nothing disturbed, hardly any noise.

When she heard Thomas break into a ground-smashing run to catch up with her, she grinned, but hid the smile before he reached her shoulder.

He said, "So you know the way to the Laird's home, do you?"

"I know the way through the mountains."

She speeded up, but with his longer legs, Thomas kept pace easily. "And how did you get out of your garden, jewel of the deep?"

Pearl hesitated before answering. Was every question from this boy a trick question?

"Over the wall."

"Very resourceful. How did you find Jasper and his horse?"

Again, she gave a short but truthful answer. "I followed the rolling ring."

"You followed it. How clever. From where?"

"From the woods."

"Why did you think it would lead you to the triplets?"

Pearl numbered the reasons on her fingers. "Because they'd left the garden on horseback, because I noticed the ring by some hoofprints, because it was obviously a piece of tack, and because it was rolling uphill all by itself, which seemed a little mysterious."

"Only a little mysterious? Do you find me a little mysterious?"

"I find you very irritating."

She could see him trying hard not to react to this insult.

"Don't you have any more questions for me?" he asked. "You were interested enough in my private business when you were eavesdropping."

"There's no point in asking questions if you can't trust the answers. Let's just find Emmie and

Ruby. So long as I get them home safe, I'm not curious about your feuds with your neighbours."

"It's not a feud. It's a battle to the death," Thomas said grimly. "And now you're involved, ignorance won't protect you."

"Then why have you involved children? Why pick my sisters and brother?"

"I didn't pick them. They were involved before they were born. It's their destiny."

"And they have no say over it?"

"Of course they do," Thomas insisted. "I want them to embrace their destiny willingly. That makes it much stronger. Jasper loves the idea of displaying his powers at a crowning ceremony."

"The girls will have much more sense."

"Will they? Don't they love being important too? Won't they want power and glory? Do you really know them better than their brother does? You don't sing their songs; perhaps you don't know them at all."

Pearl couldn't answer. She loved her sisters and brother. But Thomas was right: she didn't sing their songs, and she wasn't one of them. Perhaps they would listen to this charismatic stranger rather than their boring big sister. Perhaps they would want a destiny, even a dark one, because destiny sounded more exciting than going home for hot buttered toast.

So Pearl concentrated on the land, her gaze moving smoothly between the brittle heather at her feet and the route ahead. Thomas's eyes were moving too now, but he was glancing up and around and behind.

Pearl preferred the silence to his awkward questions and worrying answers. But as they broke away from the side of the gully to angle right towards the pass, she saw Thomas glance yet again at the sky.

She blurted out, "What are you scared of?"

"Scared? I'm not scared of anything!" he snapped.

"Then why do you keep looking round? You're like a rabbit who scents stoat."

"I'm just being careful. We're in the mountains now."

Pearl snorted. "Of course we're in the mountains! We've been climbing a mountain for the last fifteen minutes!"

"Yes, but we've crossed the line: the boundary between our land and the mountains. We could be attacked at any time."

"Attacked? Why? Is this the Laird's land already?"

"No, this is no one's land at the moment: not his, not ours. But he sometimes attacks us when we try to climb here."

"And do you attack him if he climbs here too? Or are you always the innocent victims?"

"Well, we can't let him have a chance to search for the ..." He stopped, glancing up and behind again, his eyes flicking about fast.

Pearl laughed. "Stop looking round like that!"

"Don't you like to know what's going on around you? I thought you were proud of reading the land."

"You see movement more easily out of the corner of a steady eye than if your gaze is flitting around like a butterfly. Tell me what you're looking for and I'll find it for you."

"I'm looking for the Laird's spies."

"His swans? I think even you could see a swan on a heathery hillside without all that peering and staring!"

"Not swans. He uses other birds too."

"You had pheasants dancing for you earlier. Aren't you afraid they might have been his spies?" Pearl didn't hide the scorn in her voice.

"I didn't make the pheasants dance. Jasper's song did." Thomas frowned. "I knew the triplets' powers would be different from ours, but I didn't expect dancing pheasants!" He shook his head. "Anyway, pheasants are too dim for the Laird to use as spies."

"Do you really believe that if some birds see us, they'll tell the Laird and we'll be in danger?"

"I believe it," he said firmly. "Perhaps you should believe it too, along with all the other things you've believed this morning, like rings rolling uphill."

Pearl turned round slowly. A thin scattering of tiny meadow pipits darted about to her left, and she remembered hearing the distinctive sound of a startled grouse not long ago. Tipping her head up, she saw two specks high in the sky, probably crows swooping in the air currents.

"Pipits? Grouse? Or crows?" she asked.

Thomas stopped a pace above her and shrugged. "Most likely crows, they're the cleverest and they fly furthest."

Pearl couldn't believe they were being spied on

by birds, but she had spent the morning hunting rocking horses, so perhaps it would be wise to be cautious. She looked at herself and Thomas. Her clothes had been dull enough when she put them on, and now they were camouflaged with mud. But Thomas was far too bright.

"Button your jacket to cover your red waistcoat," she instructed, "and pull the lapels up to hide your ridiculously clean shirt. If we're being hunted, we should use the land to hide ourselves, and we should stop arguing so loudly."

Thomas frowned, but he did close his jacket before they set off again up the slope.

Then Pearl's steady eye glimpsed a dark movement ahead of them. Instantly, she dropped down into the low heather.

Chapter 10

"Stop! Down!" Pearl whispered hoarsely.

Thomas stared at her, flat on the ground at his feet.

"Get down!" She tugged the hem of his jacket so he landed in the dirt, and she almost smiled as she realised that might finally take the edge of his dangerous tidiness.

Before he could yell at her, she put a finger to her lips, pointed up the hill and mouthed, "Deer."

"Deer?" He responded in a whisper because she'd spoken in a whisper. "We don't need to worry about deer. He never controls anything that doesn't fly. Come on, and stop being scared of *everything*!"

She leant close to him to whisper, "I'm not scared of deer. But if *we* scare the deer, they'll run. Then anyone, or any*thing*, watching, will know the deer have been spooked and might guess we're here. So stay down and stay quiet."

He glowered at her, but nodded once.

Now he was persuaded, she stopped using words and gestured that he must stay where he was. He rolled over and lay back casually in the heather with his arms behind his head like someone having a nap, but Pearl noticed he did it very quietly and he was careful to keep below the tops of the sparse heather.

Pearl crawled upwards, checking the wind. Even on a still day, there were always air currents around the peaks. Pearl felt a gentle current coming down the side of the Anvil. She was downwind of the herd, if they were there.

And they were. The red deer were grazing just over the next rise, hidden on the hillside far better than people with bright clothes and silver rifles. Pearl edged closer and saw a skinny stag with ten fragile points on his antlers, in the middle of his harem of eleven thin hinds and five stunted calves. This small herd wasn't as impressive as the ones she hunted on the northern mountains.

The stag kept lifting his head, sniffing the air and glancing round. The movement she'd seen was the tip of an antler swinging up and down. But his vigilance was mostly for show. Pearl searched for the oldest hinds, so old their hides were greying. They had protected many years of young, and would be the first to bolt if they suspected danger. The most alert hind was on the top edge of the herd, keeping watch with her wide-set eyes and swivelling ears.

If Pearl and Thomas were to get round the herd unnoticed, they would have to stay under the line of sight, stay silent, and stay out of the downward air current above the herd so their scent didn't reach that alert hind.

If they took the easy path, back to the left and up the side of the burn, they would be hidden by the gully, but eventually they'd have to cut across through the air current. So instead they would have to go to the right, with nothing to use as cover except the thin heather. They would have to move very slowly. Would Thomas have the patience to do that?

She crawled back towards him. He was no longer lying on his back like a cat in the sun; he was low on his stomach, his dark eyes watching her. Alert, but not like the deer watching for danger; like a predator waiting for its prey to come close.

Was she his prey?

Pearl was accustomed to being the hunter, to tracking and stalking, shooting and gralloching. She wasn't used to feeling watched and afraid.

She urged herself forward. She may not be on familiar land here, but she was used to being outdoors. Thomas spent nine months of the year at an English school. He couldn't possibly be as comfortable and skilled on moors and mountains as she was. He was no danger to her.

She moved slowly towards him, staring back at him until he blinked. Then she lay down beside him, and put her mouth to his ear. "There's an alert hind at the top of the herd, and the air is moving down the Anvil. We have to go back down a hundred yards, and up the glen to the right of them. We have to be slow and quiet."

He shook his head. She turned away so he could whisper in her ear. His breath was hot. "That will take far too long!"

"Any other way will startle them," she insisted.

"If you know so much about deer, can't you just cast a spell on them so we can walk right through the herd?" he whispered through gritted teeth.

"No. This isn't magic, it's skill. If we don't do it right, they'll tell the whole mountain range we're here. If you want to blunder through them and crash on over the pass, that's fine. You're the one who thinks we're being spied on by swans and conspired against by crows."

Thomas glared at her. Maybe he'd never been given orders by a girl before. Or maybe he'd never been given orders by someone who couldn't sing before. She shrugged and shifted slightly as if to stand up.

Thomas put his hand on her arm. "Alright. This is your lore. You got close without startling them. I probably couldn't have done that. So you lead."

They turned round and slid away from the Grey Men's Grave.

Pearl knew the best stalkers could move so carefully and so close to the ground that a deer grazing ten feet away wouldn't see the heather twitch.

Though she was well trained by Father, she wasn't an expert yet, and neither she nor Thomas were wearing proper stalking gear. But they were both slim, both supple, and both deadly serious.

So they moved slow and silent as sundial shadows, and the deer didn't notice them. But Pearl noticed growing frustration in Thomas's face every time she glanced back at him.

Pearl could move like this for hours, but Thomas was already tiring. He was having to drag his gun and that huge twisted branch along with him. Pearl considered offering to help, but she'd be delighted if he left the stick or the gun or both behind, so she just kept going.

After twenty minutes creeping through the ground cover, Pearl reached the mouth of the pass. She sat up and smiled at the deer grazing calmly below.

Then Thomas emerged from the heather beside her. He wiped his hands on the lining of his jacket and ran his fingers through his hair, picking out bits of grit and heather. He raised his silver gun and aimed at the alert hind. Then he lowered the weapon and looked at Pearl.

"Did you enjoy that, then?" he demanded.

"I enjoy a challenge."

"But who were you challenging? Yourself or me? This isn't a game."

"Are you sure it isn't a game?" She raised her eyebrows. "Aren't we playing for the future of the triplets?"

"If we are, you'll win the crawling-like-a-snake competition, but I have many other talents up my sleeve."

"Actually, you have a beetle up your sleeve."

He jerked his arms, flicking his hands at the ground, and when nothing fell out, he scowled at her.

Pearl grinned. She was truly happy for the first time since she'd heard Father's voice last night. Then she glanced behind her at the Grey Men's Grave. Still in the morning shadow of the Anvil, it looked deep and dark and cold.

Chapter 11

The shadow of the Anvil would hide Pearl and Thomas from any birds swooping in the high bright air. So, in the fewest words possible, they agreed it was safe to get up and walk through the pass.

The ground wasn't flat, but it wasn't a hard climb either, so for five minutes they walked together without arguing or racing each other.

Pearl looked up at the steep slopes of the mountains to her left and right. The huge weight of ice which had moved this way millennia ago had ripped rocks from the mountains and dragged them along, scraping out this pass. Then the glacier had thrown the rocks away.

Stepping round the moraine scattered by the ice, Pearl felt chilled. Even though it was late morning, the sun still hadn't reached into the Grey Men's Grave because the peaks either side were so high.

"Why is it called the Grey Men's Grave?" she asked. "Is anyone buried here?"

Thomas stepped in front of her and grimaced, showing all his straight white teeth. "Are you scared of ghosts?"

"I don't believe in ghosts."

"You don't have much imagination, do you?"

Pearl suddenly imagined Thomas falling face first into the slimy bog which had trapped the gold hoop, and she bit her lip to stop herself laughing. She'd enough imagination for that. Then she saw her house, empty and tidy, no triplets to annoy her. Was that her destiny?

She shook her head clear of pictures. "I was hoping for facts, not ghost stories. Do you know why it's called the Grey Men's Grave? Is it just because it's deep and dark?"

"It does feel like we're six feet under, doesn't it?" Thomas squared his shoulders to hide a sudden shiver. "I'll tell you as we walk. This isn't the list of boring facts you'd prefer, but it's the story my family tell.

"Many generations ago, the mountains were cared for by my family. So were the haughs and fields to the south and the moors and forests to the north. We had many houses and castles, but the family stronghold, where valuables and women were taken when enemies threatened, was high in the mountains."

"Valuables *and* women, indeed." Pearl snorted. "What enemies did your family have?"

"Rival clans. The English. Vikings. Romans even, long enough ago."

"Your family has always been good at annoying people, then."

He looked at her sharply, but kept speaking. "Centuries ago, Hugh Landlaw, Lord of the Mountains, Moors and Meadows, had no sons to inherit his lands and power. But his two daughters married well: both wed younger sons of families who used landlore. They were called Tam Horsburgh and Johnnie Swann.

"In order to choose his heir, Landlaw set his sons-in-law three tasks. The one who completed all three would be the next lord, holding the key to the mountains' music, as well as controlling the moors and meadows."

Pearl listened to Thomas's steady voice as they walked briskly through the pass.

"The tasks were set in the month the Lord turned fifty. The first was to prove their skills by using landlore to entertain his birthday guests. The second was to bring him a gift: either a rock from so deep in the ground that it was still burning, or a ball of snow so cold that it was still frozen in summer. The third task was to find and use the keystone which linked the family and their lore to the mountains. Only the old Lord knew exactly where it was hidden.

"They both managed the first task. Tam Horsburgh made a forest dance. The trees did an Eightsome Reel, the Gay Gordons and, of course, Strip the Willow. The Lord laughed and clapped Tam on the back. Johnnie Swann made the water in the River Stane rise up and write Happy Birthday in the air. The Lord gasped and kissed him on both cheeks."

Pearl watched Thomas as he described these fantastic events. His face was serious, like he was reciting a list of kings or other historical facts.

"Then they had to solve the riddle of the second task. Johnnie Swann found a deep hollow in this very pass, packed with snow which the sun had never warmed. He wrapped a lump the size of his head in layers of dried grass and leather. He ran all the way through the August sun to the castle of Landlaw Hold. At the feet of the Lord, he unwrapped a lump of snow the size of his fist. The Lord dropped the old cold snow into a horn cup, and drank it as it melted away.

"It looked like Johnnie had won. Because my ancestor Tam couldn't dig deep enough to find hot stones. He explored caves under the Witch's Hump at the far end of this range, and the Rhymer in the northern peaks, but the rocks there were cold and damp, not hot. He travelled on a fishing boat to Iceland, but the molten rocks he collected there were grey and hard by the time he sailed home.

"When he had only three days left, he galloped to the east coast and went deep into the ground of the Kingdom of Fife. He returned with a sack of black rocks. He laid the rocks on the stone floor, built a pile of sticks and parchment round them, and lit the kindling with a flint. The black rocks caught fire. He put his bare hand in the flames, grabbed a lump of coal, and threw it to his father-in-law, shouting out, 'It is a rock from deep in the ground, and it is glowing with heat, my Lord.' His father-in-law slapped at his smouldering cloak and laughed."

"He cheated," objected Pearl.

"That's what Johnnie Swann said. But the Lord said the last task would decide the winner. 'Race each other to find the keystone. Then we'll see who is worthy to be my heir.'

"So the next day, Tam and Johnnie kissed their

wives and baby sons goodbye and raced each other up the Keystone Peak, the highest, steepest, deadliest mountain in the county."

Pearl glanced up at the mountain on their right, bright silver in the late morning sun.

"Tam was taller and stronger on the slopes, running and leaping; at first he was in the lead. But Johnnie was like a spider up the ridge; he was in front as they neared the summit. Their wives watched the race from below. They didn't see who arrived first, nor whether either man found the stone that would make the range sing.

"All we know is that the two men fought to the death on the summit, and fell down into this pass, where they were buried for ever."

Thomas ended with a storyteller's flourish, sweeping his arm round the pass.

Pearl shook her head. "Their bodies wouldn't have rolled all the way down here! They'd have landed on the plateau or been trapped by rocks on the slopes."

"Well, that's the story we're told. That they fell here and were buried here. But there is another end to the story. I've only heard it once, not from my grandfather but from my mother, the last day she ever spoke to me. It might explain how they really ended up here in the Grey Men's Grave.

"She told me they didn't fall from the summit. They flew. They leapt off the summit together and wrestled in the air. They stabbed each other in the heart at the same moment, then fell from the sky, their arms wrapped round each other. They were buried in the same grave."

Pearl opened her mouth to ask if flying was common for people who claimed to hear the land. Then she hesitated. Would even asking the question give Thomas information he could use against the triplets?

So she asked instead, "But why the *Grey* Men's Grave? They were both young, weren't they?"

"Yes, but Tam's dark hair and Johnnie's golden hair turned silver grey in the fall from the sky."

He kept walking south. "After their husbands' deaths, the two sisters never spoke to each other again. When the old Lord died, he left the southern meadows to the Swanns, the northern moors to the Horsburghs, and the mountains to whoever could win the final task, whoever could find and use the keystone.

"But no one knows where the keystone went after the Grey Men fell. It might have fallen into the pass with them. It might still be on the summit of the peak. No one even remembers what it looks like."

They both raised their eyes. The ridged summit of the Keystone Peak neatly halved the sky above them.

"No one has sung with the mountains since, because neither family can make the link without the keystone; and neither family is safe coming here to search for it because the mountains are a no-man's land where any attack is justified.

"The war for the mountains and the search for the keystone killed many of my ancestors, and drove most of the rest away. But now it's not just the families who suffer. The mountains are suffering too. They've been neglected for so long they're starting to crumble."

Thomas turned a slow circle, gazing up at the mountains. Pearl wasn't sure if this was another piece of drama, or if he really was convinced that mountains could "suffer".

Then Pearl remembered what he'd said about his mother. "You said, the last day your mother spoke to you. Is she dead?"

"No. She was injured in an ambush meant for me, three summers ago. We hadn't even been in the mountains. It was a completely unprovoked attack. Her neck was broken. She's paralysed."

"I'm sorry," Pearl said quietly. "I'm so sorry. I didn't realise."

"You didn't realise what? That in wars, people get hurt?"

"In wars, Thomas, people *die*. My brother — who was even taller, even more handsome and even more charming than you — my brother died in the Great War. I know about wars."

"That war killed my father too. A pointless death. Fighting over land cut with so many trenches, land soaked with so much death, that no one could bear to sing with it now. At least you still have a mother and a father."

"I've already lost one brother and now you're stealing the rest of my family."

They glared at each other.

Pearl felt tears gather behind her eyes. To stop Thomas noticing, she attacked again. "Why did you let your mother get caught in an ambush meant for you? Were you lagging behind then too, looking out for feathered foes?"

"No!" Thomas swung his staff towards Pearl, but stopped the swing in time and slashed at the air instead. "We were out exercising the horses and mine fell lame. Mother cantered ahead while I walked home. Then the Laird forced the land to shift." His voice caught in his throat. "Mother was riding under the cliffs at the base of the Keystone Peak. She was caught in the rockfall.

"I heard the land roar and her horse scream at the same time. But she never made a sound. She hasn't made a sound since. We don't even know if she can hear us. All she does is breathe and swallow the soup the housekeeper spoons into her mouth. During the day her eyes are open. At night they close. But she never looks at me."

Thomas blew a long breath out, then looked at Pearl. "How did your brother die?"

"He was shot. He was armed with a pistol, and he was leading boys armed with rifles straight into machine-gun fire. Was that his destiny, do you think?" She asked the question more harshly than she'd meant, and Thomas, wisely, didn't answer.

"How did your father die?" Pearl asked in a gentler voice.

"He was blown up. His right leg was blown off, and he died while surgeons were amputating his left leg. He wouldn't have wanted to live if he couldn't walk the land. So perhaps that was his destiny."

After a silence, Pearl said, "It's not a contest, is it?"

"No."

Thomas began to walk on. Then he paused and spoke without looking back. "I don't want to hurt the triplets. Or you."

Pearl looked at the gun under his arm, and remembered his words at the gateway. "You don't want to hurt them. But you will if you have to?"

He lifted his chin to look at their path through the pass, and walked off without answering.

Chapter 12

Pearl marched through the pass, thinking about Thomas's story. She didn't believe his tale of two fighting men flying off the summit and falling out of the sky to their grave. Surely he didn't believe it either. Surely he could tell the difference between death in a story and death in a war.

She looked up at the Keystone Peak and saw a couple of crows circling above the pass. She flinched, then snorted at her own foolishness. Their black wings were flashing in the sunlight, so they must be flying above the shadow of the Anvil. Looking down from the brightness, they wouldn't be able to see Pearl and Thomas against the dark ground. Not that she really believed birds were looking for them.

Pearl took a few more steps, then looked up again to check that the birds weren't flying lower.

She was slashed across the eyes by a sudden hot pain. She cried out, ducking forward and covering her face with her hands.

The summer sun had finally reached the Grey Men's Grave. For a moment Pearl couldn't move, pinned down by the light, exposed to the sky above.

As her eyes got used to the brightness burning through her fingers and she took her hands away, she saw Thomas lift his pale face to the golden sunlight.

"Don't stand there like an idiot," Pearl yelled. "The birds can see us now!"

She scrambled over to hide in the clutter of moraine to her left. After a couple of long seconds Thomas joined her.

They looked up cautiously. The crows were still circling. Right above them.

Suddenly the crows swooped down, the tiny dots getting bigger as the birds dived towards Pearl and Thomas like they were scraps of food or shiny objects.

Pearl had a sudden vivid memory of startling a pair of crows which were pecking out the eyes of a live lamb caught in barbed wire. She felt a moment of sick fear and started scrabbling around for stones to use as weapons. But Thomas stood up and lifted his black stick towards the sky.

The crows changed course with frustrated shrieks, and flew, straight as a ruled line, through the pass and out to the Laird's land.

"Blast!" Thomas looked at his watch. "Nearly noon. I should have been checking the time." He frowned, then said firmly, "We keep going."

"But the crows saw us," Pearl pointed out. "If you're right about them, they're flying to the Laird now. So he'll know we're coming."

"The Laird has Emerald, and we want her back. I'm going on. Are you coming with me?"

Pearl didn't hesitate. "Of course I'm coming with you. I don't trust you an inch on your own." She grinned at him and took a step to the south.

But Thomas didn't follow. She turned to watch as he laid his gun down, then pushed the end of his twisted staff into the ground, tightened his right hand round the top of the staff, and placed his left hand gently on the largest rock in the jumble before him.

He began to hum, then to sing. Pearl still had no idea what the words meant, but she could hear a story in the song, about mountains reaching to the sky, about the need for height and wind and clouds. As he chanted, she realised the rock was starting to vibrate.

Thomas was singing to the mountain and the mountain was trying to sing back.

There was a grating sound, the rock moved slightly on its base and then stopped humming. Thomas took a deep breath and began again. There was no response. He tried a third time, and his voice faltered in the surrounding silence.

Thomas rested his forehead on the staff. Then he looked at the summits above him.

"I can't hear the mountains. Without the keystone, I just can't make the link. I could use my power to *force* them to my will, but I can't help them. They can't help me. I'm all alone."

His brown eyes glistened in the sunlight. "I have to find your sisters. I have to win this war." He waved the staff in a wide circle round him. "Or all this will be cold crumbling stone, and I'll have failed." His voice wavered again. He bent to pick up his gun.

Pearl wondered if he would answer the questions that were puzzling her if she asked him now, when his voice and his confidence were cracking. But it didn't seem fair to take advantage of his distress.

So she reached out and brushed his sleeve. "You're not alone. I'm here. And whether you win or lose, the mountains will still be here. It's not all your responsibility. Let's just concentrate on getting the girls back."

"You don't understand!" he snapped. "It *is* my responsibility. The pulse of the earth's music keeps the land supple. Without it, the mountains grow brittle, then crumble. They aren't just silent. They're eroding, grain by grain.

"It's started already." He pointed to a bright grey scar on the brown slope of the Anvil, so new it wasn't even on the maps in Pearl's bedroom.

"A landslip," Thomas growled. "They're happening more and more often. Cliffs breaking off, slopes covered in rubble. These mountains are barely safe now, even if you're not being attacked."

He looked at Pearl coldly. "You're just fighting for your family, but I'm fighting for the future of this land. Compared to the music of the land, children's lives are worthless. Worthless." He shook her hand off his arm and strode away.

Pearl rubbed her hand on her skirt. Perhaps she couldn't handle this boy by herself. For the first time, she considered going home and telling Mother the triplets had been stolen.

Then she imagined Mother screaming, and Father being called back from Perth with lots of logical questions. How could she explain rocking horses that galloped, rings that rolled uphill and crows that spied on climbers?

She touched the stone beside her with her fingertips. It was still cold after a night in the shadows. She hadn't really heard it sing, had she? No more than she'd ever seen people fly.

Pearl frowned. What would Peter have done if he'd found himself following a trail that started with rocking horses and led towards a war?

Would he have gone home for help, or would he have kept going, exploring new lands and finding new adventures? She had been so young when he died; she only knew him from his maps. But she knew those maps really well.

So Pearl walked fast to catch up with Thomas. They didn't speak another word as they walked to the southern mouth of the pass.

The Grey Men's Grave ended in a cliff. A new cliff, Pearl assumed, by the sharp landscape of scree and boulders at its foot. This must be one of the landslips that was making Thomas so irritable.

Then she looked past the cliff and the rock-scattered slope to the Laird's land: a land of green and blue, rather than the brown and purple they'd left behind them.

The river which curved round the base of the Anvil was broader now, fed by dozens of silver burns. White flecks were scattered on the green and the blue: sheep on the grass and swans on the water.

Pearl also saw, with a jolt of surprise, the spiralling towers and jumbled roofs of a fairytale castle. Built from pink, yellow and white stone, it was surrounded by a lacy pattern of ponds and canals, then a checked border of parklands and fields.

She grimaced. "Isn't that horrible!"

Thomas laughed harshly. "Swanhaugh Towers. The Laird's great-grandfather built it. He came back from his grand tour of Europe with a passion for German castles, French chateaux and Italian villas. But his sketches were a bit muddled."

"You think Emmie might be there? And Ruby of course."

"If they followed the river, they'll have trotted right into the Laird's front garden."

"Let's go then." Pearl turned to lower herself over the edge, but stopped, suddenly, when she saw another castle, high on side of the Anvil.

A sour grey fortress, with no more decoration than four plain round towers, one at each corner. It crouched on a sheer outcrop of rock, so the only way to reach it was by a narrow path from the slopes of the Anvil.

Pearl could see the clifftop castle was old and uncared for. The hard sun shone on cracks in the towers, and piles of tumbled stones at the base of the walls showed how much higher they'd once been. But this lump of native grey stone looked more solid than the wedding-cake castle below.

Pearl wondered why Peter hadn't put these two very different castles on his maps. Perhaps he'd felt castles weren't permanent enough to deserve a place beside mountains and rivers.

She turned to Thomas. "Is that your family's ancient stronghold?"

"Yes. Landlaw Hold."

She saw pride in his face. Not pride in himself, for once, but pride in something bigger and older.

"Do you like it?" he asked eagerly.

"It's very impressive."

"It's even more impressive inside! I've only been able to sneak in a couple of times myself. It's too close to the Laird to be safe just now, but once we've won the war I'll take you to see it." The offer was made with an open smile, but then his face closed down. "Yes. We will all go and see it soon."

Then he looked at the cliff and said with his usual smooth charm, "The fastest way down is to climb. Can you manage that?"

"Of course I can," Pearl said quickly. "But you'll not be able to carry your stick and gun. You'll need both hands. Just leave them behind a rock."

"I never leave my staff, and I should take the gun too. The Laird didn't send all his swans to your house today, and swans are bigger and braver than crows."

Thomas took off his jacket, wrapped it round the staff and the rifle, and tied the sleeves round his chest to secure the bundle to his back. "A homemade rucksack!"

As soon as he moved, the gun slid out and crashed to the ground. Pearl laughed at his surprised face, and watched as he took off the sagging jacket and tried to push the gun back inside.

Then, not wanting to waste any more time, she pulled green gardening twine from a pinafore pocket and tied the jacket tightly round the gun and stick. Thomas looked at her knots critically.

"I'll not be able to get them out fast."

"Neither will gravity."

He nodded and put the bundle back on. They peered over the edge again.

"It's not a race," announced Thomas as they examined the rock face, looking for safe handholds and footholds.

"What do you mean?" said Pearl.

"You don't have to try and prove you're a better climber than me. You might spend all your time with deer and heather, but I've spent the last couple of winters in the Alps and I don't want you going too fast to try and beat me. It's not a race."

"Of course not," agreed Pearl. "I would never be that daft."

But as she spoke, she swung herself over the edge to the first handhold she'd seen, then scrambled down the rock face. Her skirt made it hard for her to see the rock beneath her, and she hadn't planned a route all the way to the bottom, but she was sure she could find handholds and footholds.

The cliff was higher than her own four-storey house, and the ground at its base was steep and rocky. If she fell, she'd break most of her bones when she landed, and the rest as she bounced down the slope.

Pearl quickly discovered why there was so much loose stone at the bottom of the cliff. The cliff was still crumbling, the surface of the rock fragile and fracturing. She had to test each hold by pulling or stamping gently on it. But she really did want to beat Thomas, so she kept moving as fast as she could.

She glanced up at him. He was taking a route

to her right, a few yards above her. She was descending faster, because the stick and gun strapped to his back made him less agile.

Suddenly, the projecting stone supporting her left hand broke off and she swung out from the cliff. Pearl gasped, and slammed herself inwards again. She forced her left hand into the same crack as her right hand. Dust drifted out of the gap as the decaying rock began to split and shear under the increased pressure. She shifted her left foot down and around, prodding the cliff, searching for a foothold. She was past the point where she'd mapped out a route, and she couldn't look down because her arms were squashed together in front of her face.

"Are you alright?" called Thomas, still climbing steadily down.

"Yes," she grunted into her sleeves. He couldn't do anything to help anyway. Not unless she really believed he could sing the mountain solid again.

Her left foot still dangled in the air. There were no footholds. Her right foot was aching, taking almost all of her weight, and her hands were sliding out of the crowded, crumbling crack.

She looked up, saw one of the handholds she had just moved down from and jerked her left hand back up to it. Then she hung all her weight on her hands as her feet shifted back upwards to footholds she'd already tested. Now she could look for another way down.

Thomas moved smoothly past her.

"You're going the wrong way, Pearl. But don't worry. It isn't a race, after all."

Pearl felt her cheeks flare pink, and turned her head away from him. Then she traversed the cliff and followed his route down.

Thomas was waiting for her at the bottom with a gentle smile that was meant to be consoling, but made her want to punch him.

"You're shorter than me, and you're wearing a dress. You were bound to take longer."

"So it was your destiny to win and my destiny to lose, was it?" Pearl snarled.

"If you want to put it like that, yes."

"Nonsense! If that stone hadn't broken off, I would have won. That wasn't destiny, that was chance."

"It wasn't chance. You went down a fracture line, a fault in the rock. That brittle stone was going to break away as soon as any weight was put on it."

"But I might have taken a different route," she objected.

"No, you took that route because it looked the quickest from the top, and you were being hasty because you wanted to beat me. Even though it wasn't a race."

"That's not destiny. That's personality."

Thomas laughed. "Perhaps they're the same thing."

"Then how can you know Emmie and Ruby's destiny? You've never even met them."

"No, I haven't met them." Thomas turned and started down the scree. "But my grandfather made them. So he made their personalities *and* their destinies."

Pearl stared at the top of his dark head below her. What did he mean, his grandfather *made* the triplets? She thought about the three rocking horses, brought to life and controlled by the Horsburghs. Surely her brother and sisters were more real, more alive, surely they had more free will, than those unnatural horses?

Chapter 13

Thomas walked at an angle down the scree: the unstable slope of small stones which had fallen from the crumbling cliff. Pearl nodded at his choice of route. Moving sideways over the scree rather than straight down, they were less likely to slip and take a fall of loose rocks with them.

Pearl didn't try to catch up because she wasn't sure what questions she could ask about how his grandfather had "made" her sisters and brother. Anyway, she was always cautious on scree.

She remembered the first time she had been on scree, when she was much younger than the triplets were now. She'd tried to beat Father to the bottom by sitting down and sliding. But the stones had moved with her, and pulled her down too fast. When she'd tried to brake with her heels, the rock chips falling behind her started to overtake and hit her back and head. She'd reached the bottom, bruised, grazed and in tears. Father had been furious with her, and had refused to take her climbing for weeks. Even if she never climbed with Father again, she would always be careful with loose rock underfoot.

Pearl went down the scree at her own pace, placing her feet at an angle across the slope. There was no lichen or moss colouring the wide carpet of grey rock. The scree was always shifting; nothing could grow there.

She was concentrating so hard on her own footing, she didn't realise Thomas had stopped to wait for her until she nearly bumped into him.

"Don't you like walking on scree?" he asked.

"I like solid ground under my feet; not moving and rolling, certainly not humming and singing."

"I don't like scree either. It's a scar on mountains which are being worn down too fast. But we won't be on this scree much longer. It ends at those high rocks, then we follow that burn down to the Laird's grounds."

Pearl planted her feet firmly and looked ahead. Thomas was pointing at half a dozen tall pale rocks, gathered in a tight group like a quiver full of arrows. She saw a splash of red at the base of the nearest rock. Poppy red? But poppies rarely flowered this high up.

To show Thomas that her caution didn't mean she was afraid, she walked past him towards the rocks. She walked slowly; she wouldn't be pushed into unwise speed by Thomas close at her shoulder. But the scree was shifting even before she put her feet down. It seemed to be moving forwards and downwards.

No, not downwards, not straight down like gravity would move it; but diagonally down, towards the gathering of tall rocks.

Pearl tried to slow herself, but the scree kept moving. She struggled to keep her balance.

"Go back, Thomas! Get off the scree!"

She slid faster and faster downhill, remembering in her back and shoulders the pain of her crashing descent years ago. Then she heard a harsh grinding sound over the clattering of small stones under her feet. The noise was coming from the rocks ahead.

She looked up, her arms flapping as she tried to stay on her feet. The patch of poppy red had spread, like liquid, all round the rocks.

And the rocks were grinding against each other, turning in the ground as though giant hands under the earth were twisting them. The rocks stood so close together, they struck sparks off each other as they moved.

Pearl jerked back with horror, lost her balance and sprawled on the tide of stones dragging her down.

As she slid closer, the smallest stones bouncing past her were caught between the two nearest rocks and crushed into dust.

She dug her heels and hands into the scree, ripping nails and skin in a frantic attempt to slow herself down. But she couldn't grasp solid ground beneath her, just the tumbling current of stones taking her nearer and nearer to the grinding rocks.

She twisted her head. Was Thomas being dragged behind her?

He was on the shifting scree too, but he had his right hand over his left shoulder, trying to free his staff. Finally he managed to tug it out from the bundle on his back. In one smooth arc he thrust it straight through the scree into the thin earth beneath. It was enough to stop his slide, and Pearl watched as he leapt off the narrow band of moving stones onto a safe part of the slope.

"Pearl!" he shouted, his face white and his eyes dark.

"I can't stop!" she screamed, now only yards from the groaning rocks.

She could feel the heat from the sparks below. She could smell the stink of spilled blood. She couldn't hear Thomas any more. All she could hear was the thundering of the rocks. All she could see was a cloud of dust.

The solid shapes of the grinding rocks loomed out of the grey air ahead of her. Pearl straightened her trembling legs and pointed the soles of her strong black boots at the two leading rocks.

Her feet hit the rocks and she braced herself against the pull of the stones beneath her. The rocks held her up against the current of scree, but it was a temporary safety. The turning surfaces were dragging her boots inwards to the tiny crushing gap between them.

So she lifted her left foot, putting her whole weight on her right for a moment, and moved her left away from the gap. Then she lifted and moved her right foot. For a few moments Pearl lay on the slope, dancing a gritty two-step with the grinding rocks.

But the soles of her boots were wearing away, her legs were tiring and her back was being scraped raw by the stones underneath.

She risked a glance up. Where was Thomas?

He was standing on safe solid ground, watching her fight for her life.

Pearl could hardly breathe or think. She forced all her strength into her legs and feet. She could hold herself here for a little while longer, but the boy above was her only hope of rescue.

Even through the dust she could see he was scowling, arguing with himself. Then suddenly he stepped to the very edge of the moving stones. He thrust the staff into the slope again, and threw himself onto the river of scree. He lost his footing immediately, but the staff held firm and he didn't slide down. He twisted round and held out his left hand towards Pearl.

"Take my hand!"

Pearl couldn't reach, not with both feet braced against the rocks.

His long fingers stretched towards her.

"I can't get any closer. Grab my hand, Pearl."

This was her only chance. She lifted her left foot off the rock below, pushed as hard as she could with her right foot and launched her hand at his. He grabbed her wrist, as she felt her right foot slip towards the crushing gap.

Thomas pulled her up a couple of inches.

She could see the strain in his face. Her arm felt like it was being ripped apart at elbow and shoulder, and the scree was still battering at her body. But Thomas's grip was strong, and she didn't slip back towards the rocks.

He shifted slowly up the slope, using the staff to pull himself off the scree, dragging Pearl up with him. As she dangled from his hand, she swung round so the scree was sliding under her stomach.

Thomas stopped for a few deep breaths once he was on calm ground. His long arm was still holding

Pearl over the moving stones, above the grinding rocks.

She waited for him to get his breath back and pull her right up. But his eyes narrowed, and he spoke very clearly over the harsh noise below.

"Where is Ruby?"

Pearl gasped. "What?"

"Where is Ruby?"

Through eyes watery with dust and fear, she stared at him. It had been a race, a contest, a war all along. And she had lost.

"Where is Ruby?"

There was no point in denying that she knew the answer, that she had rescued her sister and hidden her. He must have known since she followed the ring, since the rocking horse attacked her. He'd always known; that's why he'd taken her with him. But she didn't have to give him the answer he wanted.

"I won't tell you." She threw the hard words into the air between them.

"I'm holding your life in my hand, quiet girl. Tell me, where is Ruby?"

The rocks were grinding so loud that Pearl could hardly remember who her sister was, nor why she loved her. The endless rolling stones were scraping the courage from her body. But Pearl groaned, "I will not ... betray ... my sister."

Thomas almost screamed, "Where is she? Tell me. I can't hold you for ever."

She couldn't say it again. She just shook her aching head.

"It's your choice, Pearl. I can pull you up or let

you go. It's your choice."

Her dry mouth croaked, "No, Thomas. It's your choice."

He closed his eyes briefly, then laughed.

Just as she expected his fingers to open and drop her, he gave a hoarse yell, and heaved her onto the calm earth round the staff.

As soon as they were both off the scree, the grinding slowed and stopped.

Now the grit and dust were settling, Pearl could see a hare sitting on top of the middle rock. No, the hare was at too odd an angle. It was a corpse, propped up on the rock. A dead hare, ears dangling and paws open wide in a comic question.

Had it been hare's blood she'd smelt at the foot of the rocks? Was this the Laird's bloodlore?

She looked away from the rocks. Battered and shocked, she didn't want to sit up, or stand up, or walk on. And she really didn't want to speak to Thomas.

But she hauled herself over to the tiny burn falling down to the Laird's lands. She rinsed the warmth of Thomas's hand from her wrist, the grit from her palms and the blood from her nails. She drank handfuls of cold clean water.

She looked at Thomas. He was sitting with his arms round his knees, looking down at the castle and canals below.

He said quietly, "We will still find Ruby. But if we find her without you, then you won't be able to offer her a different destiny. You've shown your bravery, Pearl, now show some sense and tell me where she is."

Pearl shook her head, still rattling with the remains of her terror. "You were prepared to kill me!"

"I threatened to kill you. That's different."

"It didn't feel different."

He waved his hands at the hare and the bloodstained rocks. "It ends differently."

"Would you do anything to get these mountains for your family?"

"Yes. Anything. I'll do anything to win. I'll reward those who help me, and grind down those who don't. Are you still with me?"

"No, Thomas. I was never really with you. But I am going down there to get Emmie. If you're going too, we'll go the same way. But not together. Not ever again."

Pearl stood up slowly. Every muscle in her body ached and her skin stung with grazes, but she climbed down the side of the burn as it splashed round the edge of the scree. She heard Thomas take a quick drink then follow her.

As she moved down the hill, faster and stronger with every step, she wondered how she could save her sister from both the Laird ahead of her and the boy behind her.

Chapter 14

Pearl stayed ahead of Thomas until they reached the bottom of the slope. But then she had to stop.

From the cliff, the land round the castle had seemed open: sweeping lawns decorated by curls of water. Pearl hadn't noticed the thin dark shadow of a wall, drawing a line between the barren mountains and the Laird's green parklands.

Now the wall was blocking her way. The top was higher than her arms could stretch, and the stones fitted so close together they gave no holds for climbing. She slumped against the wall and sighed. She was almost too sore and too tired to keep going.

Thomas arrived beside her.

"Shall we work together?" he asked in a smooth voice. "Just for a moment? Just to get over the wall?"

She swung round to him and yelled, "I don't like you and I don't trust you and I will not let you have my sister!"

"I know. But will you help me over the wall?"

"Me, help you! You must be joking." She considered the height of the wall. "You could give me a boost; I'm lighter."

"No!" Thomas laughed. "If I help you up, you'll leave me here."

"But if I help *you* up, you'll leave *me* here."

"No, I won't. I still need you to reassure Emerald. I'll need all my energy for the Laird, so you can comfort her or brush her hair or whatever little girls need. That's why I let you tag along, remember." He was adjusting the bundle on his back, securing the staff and gun.

"No it isn't, you talked me into coming because you wanted to find out where Ruby was. That's all." Pearl kicked the base of the wall.

"That too. But I do want you to come to Swanhaugh Towers. Perhaps if you meet the Laird, you'll think better of me."

"I've seen his castle, Thomas. I already like him even less than I like you."

"Help me up, Pearl, and I promise I will pull you up after me."

"Why would I believe a promise from you?"

Thomas gripped Pearl's shoulders and looked into her eyes. "By the land's music and by my forefathers' lore, I give you my word I will get you over the wall."

Pearl nodded. She would have to take the chance.

She linked her hands to make a stirrup and braced her back against the wall. They both took a deep breath. Thomas put his left foot in her hands and she threw him upwards as he leapt. She stumbled as his weight left her palms.

Thomas pulled himself to the top of the wall, then, without a moment's hesitation, he leant down, his long fingers reaching for Pearl's hand. She shivered at the idea of trusting herself to that strong grasp again. But she reached up, he grabbed her tightly and lifted her up beside him.

"Thank you," they both said, politely, at the same time. Thomas grinned. Pearl frowned.

"You didn't use such a strong oath when you promised I could offer the triplets an alternative to your destiny."

"No, I didn't." He raised his eyebrows and his smile grew wider.

"Will you swear now, by the oath I can believe, the oath you've just used, that I can have my say before you ask them to follow you?"

"No," he said bluntly as he slid down the wall to the grass beneath.

"Why not?" she demanded, following him down.

He dismantled the bundle, put the jacket on, straightened his cuffs and hem, and armed himself again with the gun and the twisted stick.

"Because the Laird knows we're coming. There might be no time to listen to my stories and songs, or your facts and arguments. Everyone's destiny is approaching fast. It might be too late for anyone to choose."

He turned his back on her and ran across the grass towards the nursery colours of Swanhaugh Towers.

Pearl patted her pockets, hoping to find a weapon, then set off after him.

The castle didn't look any better close up. As she ran nearer, it began to look even worse. The walls were white stone, but the towers, the columns, the lintels, the balconies and the gargoyles were all carved from buttery yellow or sugary pink stone. It looked as if it was built to be eaten. Pearl felt like Gretel heading for the gingerbread house. Was there a witch inside? Would she bother to save this maddening Hansel from the oven?

If this fancy castle had been baked and iced, it was getting stale. It wasn't aging like the castle she'd seen on the cliffs. It was rotting and mouldering. The pastel colours were smeared with streaks of mucus green from old copper and blood red from rusting iron. Ragged curtains drifted out of cracked windows.

The land around wasn't well tended either. The grass under her feet was long and lush, but it was growing in clumps like wild grass, not like a smooth garden lawn.

The sheep in the fenced off fields towards the river were plump enough, but they hadn't been shorn last spring and their fleeces looked ragged and hot.

And the intricate canals looping round the castle were full of thick weed and bright green algae.

Thomas sprinted across the canals on slimy stepping stones, not slackening his pace at all, and Pearl followed as fast as she could.

She was about to cross the widest strip of smelly water when she heard a whooping booming noise. A dozen swans swooped through the air above them.

Thomas skidded to a halt on the grass, raised his gun and fired. A swan fell out of the air into the canal, filthy water splashing Pearl's shins. She looked at the twisted white neck and dark eye, sinking below the fragile surface of the water. A dragonfly glittered above the bird's open beak.

Pearl had only ever seen animals shot in sport before, never in hate or anger or fear. It didn't seem right. There were rules in sport, but there weren't any rules today.

The other swans wheeled away, and Thomas fired again, bringing down another bird.

Pearl watched him as he balanced on the balls of his feet, calmly swinging the gun round like part of his arm. Perhaps he wasn't shooting in fear, or anger, or hate. This was a war, and Thomas might have the skill, power and coolness to win. Unfortunately, Pearl didn't think they were on the same side.

She skidded across the stepping stones and caught up with him as he reloaded. The remaining swans circled behind the castle.

"Well done," she said. Thomas gave her a smug smile. "Well done," she repeated, "now everyone knows we're here."

He scowled. "The Laird knows already; the crows will have told him we're on our way. But he doesn't know the strength of my powers, nor the depth of your thrawn bloodymindedness, so we can still surprise him."

He ran on towards the castle. Pearl followed, a few steps behind.

"Have you been here before?" she called after him.

"No!"

"Do you know where you're going?"

"No!"

"Do you know where the Laird and Emmie will be?" At least she didn't have to keep pretending

Ruby was here too.

"No!" he shouted back. "But if we make enough noise, I'm sure they'll come to us."

Pearl shook her head in astonishment. Then she brought Thomas to a halt by accelerating and getting in front of him.

"That's a dreadful tactic. You throw away all our advantages that way."

"What do you suggest, then?"

"We haven't been invited. It would be rude to go in the front door, so let's find the back way in. Then follow our noses, our eyes and our ears."

"Follow them to what exactly?" he asked impatiently.

"To whatever trouble Emmie is causing the Laird."

"Trouble? She's only ten years old. He's a powerful and skilled lord of the land. She won't be causing him any trouble."

"You don't know Emmie. If we get in there, I'll find her."

To her surprise, he didn't argue. He nodded. "That's why you're here." So he ran towards the northern corner of Swanhaugh Towers, rather than the arched and pillared front door.

They sprinted round the side of the north wing, and found a jumble of outbuildings, stables and sheds forming a rough courtyard against the back wall of the castle.

There were four back doors into the main building. Pearl guessed they would lead to the kitchen, the cellars, the gunroom and the servants' quarters.

Every door was closed, and every door was guarded by two or three swans. Not elegant as they were on the water, nor wide and swooping as they were in the air, but squat-bodied, snake-necked and menacing.

Chapter 15

Thomas and Pearl faced the barrier of swans.

He lowered the muzzle of his silver gun. "I can't shoot them all."

"Why not?" Pearl's sympathy for the swan in the canal dissolved at the sight of these malignant birds between her and her sister.

"I don't have enough bullets."

Pearl counted the swans in the courtyard.

"You didn't bring a dozen bullets with you! What kind of war are you running here?"

"I'd need more than a dozen. Look up."

About thirty swans were looping in a wide oval above them, and more were arriving, in twos and threes, from all over the estate.

"There are already too many for me to fend off with my gun or my staff."

"Sorry," Pearl said. "We should have gone to the front door after all."

"Never mind. It's probably locked anyway."

Pearl examined the back of the castle. She and Thomas could easily climb the crumbling wall to the first floor windows, but they wouldn't escape from winged enemies by going upwards.

Downwards then? She saw the grimy hatch of a coal cellar, but it was blocked by swans too.

No, the easiest thing was just to walk in through the back door.

"Are they real swans?" Pearl asked suddenly.

"What?"

"Are they actual swans? Apart from doing what the Laird wants, do they act like real swans?"

"Yes." Thomas sounded puzzled. "But even ordinary swans are violent when they're defending their territory."

"I have a plan," she said quietly. "We're aiming for the nearest door. It has a glass pane at the top, so even if it's locked, you can smash the glass and unlock it. I'll distract them. You break in."

Pearl began to walk slowly towards the three swans guarding the nearest door.

Thomas lifted the gun and followed her.

"Lower the gun," she ordered.

She slipped her hand into the biggest pocket of her pinafore. When she'd searched for weapons as they entered the Laird's park, she hadn't found a dagger or a pistol or any undetectable poison, but she had found something much more useful against swans.

She pulled out a soft packet, unwrapped it and started to tear the contents into small lumps. Then, like a gardener sowing seeds, she swung her hand round, opened her fingers and cast dozens of jammy breadcrumbs onto the ground over to her right.

The swans stared at the bread, then one by one they lifted their heads and stared at Pearl.

If they went for her rather than the sandwich, she had nothing to defend herself with. She scattered more crumbs.

The first swan broke, rushing to get to the food before the others.

The second swan blundered after the first. They started hissing and barging each other out of the way as their bright orange beaks scooped up the breadcrumbs.

That left only one swan, a huge cob, standing directly between her and the door.

Pearl lifted the last sandwich and waved it at the remaining swan. Its tiny black eyes, hidden in the black feathers round its beak, watched the moving bread. She waved it further. The swan's head and neck began to swing with the bread. Pearl flung the sandwich over the heads of the squabbling swans, further away from the door.

The third swan crashed after the bread. Thomas threw his staff like a spear through the glass pane. He reached the door in four long strides, shoved his arm over the jagged glass and opened it from behind. He leapt across the doorstep and inside.

Pearl walked calmly past two swans gobbling breadcrumbs. The third swan, with a triangular sandwich in its beak, flapped back towards her. Thomas grabbed her arm, pulled her in and slammed the door.

"Feeding the enemy?" he said sternly, then laughed. "That was clever! What else do you have in those pockets?"

"Nothing much." Pearl heard a skyful of swans landing angrily outside. "Can they get through the door?"

Thomas locked the door. Then he poked a finger through a rip in the sleeve of his tweed jacket.

"They'll not risk their necks on that sharp glass, and anyway, they can't work the lock. We're safe from swans while we're inside."

He smiled at her. "We work well together, Pearl Chayne."

"Only when we want the same thing."

"Now we both want Emerald. Let's go and get her."

They ran into a dark kitchen, past a wide cold oven and rows of copper pans hung on hooks in order of size. Pearl dropped the jammy paper wrapper on a scarred wooden table. She wondered if cooks had stuffed swans on it in the olden days.

They sprinted along a dingy servants' corridor and through a swing door into the entrance hall, then slid to a halt on the tiled floor.

The air was chilly and musty, and Pearl's footsteps echoed as she walked to the middle of the black and white tiles. She saw padlocks and chains hanging on the back of the huge front door. They couldn't have got in that way after all.

Opposite the door, a staircase swept up, curving several times round the sides of the oval hall. Pearl squinted up and counted five floors above. The balconies and landings were dimly lit through a glass ceiling, spotted with dirt.

Pearl walked round, looking at a three-legged table with a silver tray for calling cards, though no one had called recently except dead flies; a chest of drawers topped by a bronze bust of a famous Scottish writer, whose name Pearl couldn't remember, with yellowing envelopes tucked under his chin; a tilting coatstand holding a wide hat trimmed with white feathers, and a couple of motheaten velvet coats; and a cracked glass dome in an alcove, filled with stuffed birds: capercaillies and humming birds, woodpeckers and falcons, their wings fluffy with dust.

"Knowing landlore hasn't made the Laird rich or popular, has it?" she murmured.

"That's because he spends his time getting high on the smell of blood," Thomas answered. "He only cares about his own pleasures, not about the health of his land or the weight of his purse."

Thomas leant against the bottom post of the banister, watching Pearl as she knelt down to look at the worn tiles behind the front door.

"My dear girl, are you really trying to use your low poacher's tracking skills *inside* the castle?"

Pearl didn't answer. She counted the doors off the central hall. As well as the narrow swing doors that led to the servants' corridors, there were four double wooden doors, heavy and carved.

She pushed gently at one. It creaked open, revealing a room full of stiff armchairs, facing a wide window looking out at the canals. "Parlour," she muttered.

The next room had a huge table, a stone fireplace and dozens of wooden chairs. "Dining room."

The third contained just two chairs, but hundreds of bookshelves. "Library."

The last door was locked. She put her ear against the wood, but heard nothing except Thomas's impatient sighs behind her.

She walked round the hall again, measuring the width of the narrow doorways with her arms. She stood beside Thomas, looking at the first few steps of the staircase. Then she ran to the unlocked doors and looked at those rooms once more.

The library's highest bookshelves were on a gallery halfway up the walls. The parlour and the dining room were ringed with balconies for servants to light the chandeliers hanging from the high ceilings.

"There's another entrance to this locked room one floor up," Pearl announced. "We have to go up those stairs to find Emmie."

"How do you know she's in there?"

"Because it's the only locked door which is wide enough to let a horse through."

Thomas laughed. "Why does the width of the door matter?"

"Because there are wet hoofprints behind the front door."

Thomas rushed over. Three distinct hoofprints were just visible, the damp shapes taking a long time to dry in this cold atmosphere. He cleared his throat, but Pearl had no time for apologies.

"Could the horse go up the stairs without ripping or marking the carpet?" she demanded.

"No."

"Are the servants' doors wide enough to let a horse through?"

"No."

"Then Emmie, or her horse at least, is behind that locked door. And there's a balcony in every other room, so let's go up and get onto the balcony of this room."

Thomas followed Pearl, two steps at a time, up

the sweeping staircase to a single door directly above the locked double entrance in the hall. They put their shoulders to the door, shoved at it, then stumbled in when it opened easily.

They found themselves standing in deep shadow on a narrow gallery, above a huge high room furnished with nothing but faded couches round the edges of a wooden floor. The gallery widened at one end into a platform, cluttered with rusty music stands.

"Ballroom," muttered Thomas.

"Minstrels' gallery," murmured Pearl.

But neither of them were really looking at the details of the room. They were staring at the people in the centre of the room.

Pearl wondered if the two people in front of them were playing a game. The child was giggling, but the man was cursing under his breath. He was chasing the girl, trying to grab her arm, her dress, her foot. She was eluding him, moving faster, making sharper turns, ducking and somersaulting, always an inch away from his grasping fingers.

Pearl held her breath as they raced up and down the ballroom. The man was skinny, wearing a purple velvet suit and a lacy shirt, his white hair tied back with a ribbon. He moved smoothly, skilfully, but without the speed and agility of his young quarry.

The girl had curly blonde hair and a dark green cotton dress. Her cheeks were pink with effort and laughter.

And she swooped through the air in front

of Pearl and Thomas, chased by the man with flapping coat-tails and long bony arms.

Emmie and the Laird. Both moving like birds through the air, or fish through the sea. No wires or ropes or wings. Just swooping and diving and floating and flying.

Chapter 16

"She can *fly!*" whispered Thomas. "She can *fly!*"

He turned to Pearl, his face pale and clammy, looking as if he'd found maggots under his tongue.

"She can *fly!* Why didn't you tell me?"

The chase sped under the minstrels' gallery. The Laird rose straight up so fast that he banged his head on the wooden underside of the platform. This time Pearl heard him curse out loud.

She grinned. "I didn't tell you because I didn't know. But I did know she would be more than a match for the Laird. And for you and all your wooden horses."

"How could you not know? She must have been practising. Look at that, for goodness sake." Emmie was cartwheeling along the ceiling.

"Well, I wasn't sure. When Ruby and Jasper fly they usually make a mess of it and end up trapped on wardrobes or dangling from doocots. I don't have to rescue Emmie nearly as often, so I guessed she might be better at it."

"The others fly too?" Thomas asked faintly.

Pearl peered over the edge of the gallery to watch the Laird chase Emmie along the floor, both gliding a nail's breadth above the bare boards. They swerved up the wall beside the vast fireplace at the other end of the ballroom.

"Yes, they fly too. Why? Don't you want them now?" Pearl's quiet voice was teasing. "Are flying children not part of your grand plan?"

"I suppose the more powers they have, the stronger the crown will be. But the Horsburghs haven't flown since Tam Horsburgh fell to his death. It's a Swann power. Just like the birds reacting to Jasper's singing. It may mean …" His voice faded away.

"It may mean what?"

"It may mean my grandfather wasn't the only one who thought of creating children to be the jewels in our crown."

"How did he create them, exactly?" Pearl asked. "What does he want them for? They're children, not a magical experiment. Tell me what you mean when you say he *created* them!"

"Not now. No time. We have to rescue her."

He raised his staff and aimed it at the pair floating in front of the high windows. Emmie was bobbing in the air with her arms crossed and a grin on her porcelain doll's face, moving just enough to avoid the bony arms stretching for her.

Pearl cracked the edge of her hand against Thomas's wrist and the staff fell. "No! She doesn't need rescuing. Not by you."

As Thomas bent to pick up his stick, they heard a clatter below them.

Thomas curled his upper body right over the panelled side of the gallery, to see the floor directly beneath. Then he uncurled and beckoned Pearl to join him. She didn't entirely trust him not to pitch her over, so she knelt down and looked through a gap in the floorboards. She glimpsed a white shape, catching the light on its varnished curves.

"Emmie's horse?" Pearl asked.

"Yes. The poor thing's chained up, she's terrified, and she's wearing herself to splinters trying to escape. I have to rescue her as well as Emerald."

"Are the rocking horses really alive then? Do they have feelings?"

"Of course. Once anything is alive it has a full set of feelings and a strong hold on life. I'm responsible for that horse," insisted Thomas, "so I can't just leave her here."

Pearl looked up at Emmie, flying near the ceiling, slowing down to fool the Laird into making a careless grab, then jinking out of his reach.

"She's trying to tire him out," said Pearl.

"Shouldn't we let her know we're here?"

Pearl chuckled. "She knows."

"What makes you think that? We're standing in shadow, we're whispering and she hasn't looked in this direction, nor has the Laird."

"Of course she knows we're here. Look, she's showing off."

Emmie was spinning and twisting in the air: first like a seed pod falling from a sycamore tree, then a coin in a magician's hand, then a flame in the wind.

Thomas sighed. "That's how I would fly if I could. She's amazing, isn't she?"

"She's a very cheeky little girl, and I need to get her home for her lunch." Pearl was smiling broadly.

"But what a power to harness!"

"It's not your power. It's her power, to use however she wants."

"But my grandfather created her."

"Really? Did he create a child who could fly?"

While Emmie concentrated on her dance, the Laird was crawling silently through the air towards her.

"Look out!" yelled Thomas. "Behind you!"

Emmie laughed, and shrank from a tall twisting flame to a tiny bouncing ball by wrapping her arms round her knees, so the Laird slipped right under her.

Then she swam through the air and popped up at the gallery, vaulting over to land at Pearl's side.

"Hello Pearl! Did you follow the horse? Have you been watching me fly?"

"You looked very fancy, Emmie. Come on, we need to get home."

The Laird hauled himself over the rail, and stood a few steps away with his hand pressed to his chest, getting his breath back.

Thomas stepped heroically between the girls and the man, and lifted his staff.

Now the Laird was so close, Pearl could see he wasn't as dapper as he'd looked in the air. His purple velvet suit was faded and missing a few buttons. His white hair was greasy at the scalp and tinged with yellow at the ends. His shirt had food stains on its throat ruffles and splatters of dark red on its frayed cuffs.

The Laird slid his left fingers up his right sleeve to pull out a smooth white stick as long as his forearm. A bone, with black and white feathers lashed to one end by a piece of leather. He pointed it at Thomas.

"Oh, don't be daft!" Emmie darted out in front of Thomas and stood between the two of them.

"Put your toys down. If you fling spells at each other you might hurt me and you don't want to do that, do you?"

She stood with her hands on her hips and her head cocked, and she smiled as the man and the boy did exactly as she ordered.

"Now," she turned to Thomas, "perhaps you should introduce yourself, as my sister is usually too busy watching and thinking to be polite."

Pearl was watching her sister's confident stance, and thinking it was going to be difficult to rescue someone who believed she was in charge. Emmie didn't know how dangerous this war had become. Pearl's back and legs twitched as she remembered the scree and the grinding rocks.

Thomas smiled his most charming smile, and spoke in his most alluring voice. "I am Thomas Horsburgh, and I have come over the mountains for you, Emerald Chayne."

"Don't call me Emerald Chayne; it makes me sound like a trinket. Call me Emmie."

"Emmie, you must come with me and your sister, because this man wants to harm you."

"And what do you want, Thomas Horsburgh?"

"I want you to fulfil your destiny. I want you, Ruby and Jasper to crown my grandfather Lord of the Mountains, then share in his glory for ever."

Emmie laughed.

So did the Laird.

They stood in a line along the gallery: Emmie between the Laird and Thomas, then Pearl behind Thomas, ignored by the other three, watching and waiting for a chance to grab her sister.

The Laird spoke. His voice wasn't deep and musical like Thomas's, it was sharper and oilier, but it wound round Pearl's head and into her ears.

"Don't trust him, Emmie. He wants to waste all your lovely power and potential, just to make his old fossil of a grandfather happy for a few years.

"Why is that, Thomas? Why is your grandfather's crown so important to you? What has he promised you, boy? You won't be content with moors, mountains and meadows. You're far more ambitious. So why this fuss over the triplets, their horses and your grandfather's crown?

"You've already guessed, Emmie, that I'm up to no good, but don't let his pretty face fool you. He's just as ruthless as I am, and even more hungry for power."

Pearl, standing behind Thomas, saw his shoulders tense. The Laird smiled, showing a mouth full of grey teeth.

"I would be honest with you and the other little darlings, Emmie. I would explain the full crowning ceremony. But will he tell you the truth? Before he rescues you from my terrible claws into his nice clean hands, ask him how his ceremony *ends*!"

"So, Thomas," asked Emmie in her light cheerful voice, "tell me about your ceremony."

Thomas took a deep breath. "You can hear the land, can't you? You can sing with the land?"

He paused and looked at Emmie hopefully. She nodded and raised her eyebrows.

"This ceremony will bring you even closer to the land. You will be part of a power that will link us to the mountains for ever."

Emmie smiled sweetly. "That sounds nice."

Pearl saw Thomas relax his shoulders. Her own hands were in fists so tight she could feel her nails bending against her palms.

Emmie, still smiling sweetly, asked, "But how does it end?"

There was silence. Pearl's hands softened.

"Afterwards, can we go home and have tea?"

Thomas was still silent.

Emmie spoke even more softly. "Pearl? What do you think? Do you trust him?"

"I don't trust either of them. I think you make your own destiny, you don't let others choose it for you. Come on, Emmie, let's go and get Jasper and Ruby, then we can all go home."

Pearl held her hand out to Emmie, who took one step towards her.

"NO!" shouted the Laird and Thomas. They both raised their weapons again.

Emmie was still smiling. "Don't you both need me alive?"

But Thomas smiled too, his wolfish long-toothed smile, not charming at all. "You aren't tall enough or wide enough to protect Swanhaugh from me, little girl." He laughed and began to twist his staff. "You'd need to be as big as a mountain to be a barrier between a Horsburgh and a Swann once we start to fight. And when I've defeated him, I'll have you all to myself."

He swung his staff in an arc, aiming it just above Emmie's head.

At first Pearl thought Thomas's attack had failed. She couldn't see sparks or light or anything else magical flying out of the end of his staff.

But then a deep boom filled the ballroom, and the Laird fell backwards. He staggered upright again and swept his bone baton through the air towards Thomas, who ducked as a high-pitched rattle crashed round the room. A crack appeared in the wall at the other end of the gallery.

"Oooooh!" shrieked Emmie theatrically and flung herself past Thomas into Pearl's arms.

"Cower down," Emmie muttered. "Look scared."

"I am scared!" hissed Pearl. "What are they doing?"

"The Laird told me they store sound energy from the land in those sticks ..." The girls crouched down as Thomas and the Laird threw more bolts of sound at each other. The gallery shook as each boom and rattle collided.

"They should save that energy to care for the land," Emmie whispered. "Instead they're just chucking it at each other. What a waste. But look at them. Amazing! I wonder if I could learn to do that?"

As the duel moved further down the gallery, Pearl edged towards the door. But Emmie didn't follow. The next boom knocked both of them against the wall.

As Pearl pulled herself up, she wondered who would win this deafening duel. The Laird could fly

132

to escape Thomas's blasts, but his return attacks
weren't as strong. Thomas's low booms rocked the
whole ballroom; the Laird's painful rattles only
made eggshell cracks in the plaster.

When the Laird hit Thomas, the boy braced
himself against the blows and stood firm; when
Thomas hit the Laird, the man was knocked
sideways and grimaced in pain.

Pearl tugged Emmie's sleeve. "Why are we
cowering? Why aren't we running?"

"I want to watch. And if they think we're poor
wee things, they'll ignore us. Then when we do
leave, they'll take longer to notice. So sniffle a bit
when there's silence."

"Stop being so melodramatic, Emmie! They're
fighting for their lives. They won't notice a bit of
play-acting. As soon as they move to the other end
of the gallery, we're leaving. Fast."

Emmie nodded reluctantly. Pearl balanced on
her toes, ready to run.

Thomas was still too close to them, leaning over
the railing to throw another echoing boom towards
the Laird. The Laird flapped upwards and flung
another rattle at Thomas. Thomas leapt out of the
way, but the leading edge of the sound caught his
gun, crushing the silver barrel.

Thomas dropped the gun over the edge. It
wasn't the weapon he chose to fight with. Then he
raced past Pearl and Emmie to the far side of the
gallery, holding his staff high.

They dashed through the open door and down
the stairs, hand in hand.

Chapter 17

Pearl and Emmie leapt off the bottom step, slid across the tiled hall and ran through the swinging servants' door.

As they clattered onto the stone floor of the kitchen, Pearl slowed and looked round. She couldn't see any knives, and didn't have time to search through drawers, so she unhooked a heavy copper pan from the wall.

"Take one, Emmie. We might need to fight off swans."

Armed with a frying pan and a saucepan, they walked quietly towards the back door.

Pearl stood on tiptoe to peer through the jagged hole in the glass. No white feathers, no orange beaks. She clicked the latch and opened the door slightly, just enough to see out, her body braced to slam it shut. But the courtyard was empty.

"Come on!" She opened the door wide.

"Do we still need these?" Emmie waved her little pan. "Are we having a campfire?"

"Don't be silly. Keep hold of it for now, in case they're waiting round the corner."

And they were. Dozens of bickering swans, with weaving necks and stabbing beaks, waiting to ambush anyone leaving the courtyard. Pearl pulled back before they noticed her and whispered, "We'll have to go round the other way."

They ran back across the courtyard, and after peering into several rickety sheds, found a garage with a broken car and an open back door. They slipped through onto a gravelled road leading round the side and front of the castle.

Pearl led them round the south west corner, pan held high, but there were no swans waiting.

They crept along the wall of the castle, until they came to a row of tall greasy windows.

"These are the ballroom windows," whispered Pearl. "Don't look in, just duck down and keep going."

Emmie nodded. Pearl crouched low and crawled below the first window ledge. Suddenly, the window swung open above her, and a purple sleeve thrust out over her head, so she scrambled back again.

Pearl bumped into Emmie's knees as they heard the Laird screech, "I may not be able to defeat you with the power in my old bones, but I will defeat you with blood."

They heard Thomas answer, clear but faint from inside the castle, "Bloodlore has less power than you think; it draws from you as well as gives to you."

"Then why are you backing away, boy?"

Pearl and Emmie held their breath as the Laird leant forward and drove his bone staff into the ground.

There was a massive crashing boom, and glass exploded onto the grass. Thomas had shattered the window.

"Ha!" yelled the Laird. "Thank you!"

His white hand picked up a triangle of glass and vanished back into the room. Pearl heard a short squeal, then the Laird leant his whole torso out of the window.

Both girls pressed themselves against the stained, damp wall, but the Laird wasn't looking in their direction. He was staring at his hands, wrapped round a brown wriggling shape.

Suddenly he twisted his hands, turning them in opposite directions, wringing the shape like a wet sock, squeezing a jet of bright blood towards the upright bone. Most of the red shower splattered onto the grass, but plenty of blood struck the bone and slid in thick drops down its white length.

While the Laird twisted his hands, Pearl saw a hairless pink tail slip between his knuckles. A rat's tail. The tail jerked twice, then went limp.

As he drained the rat of blood, the Laird was chanting, like Thomas had chanted to the rock, but higher, sharper, more demanding. There was a rumble, a deep sound from deep underground.

Pearl grabbed Emmie's hand.

The Laird stopped singing and dropped the rat to the ground. He lifted his left hand to his mouth and licked his thumb, then ripped the bone out of the earth, a spray of red following it through the air.

He whirled back into the ballroom, yelling, "NOW feel the power of the earth, boy!" A huge vibrating clatter, like the rattles he'd produced before but ten times louder, juddered around the castle.

The Laird laughed and began to chant again, and Pearl became aware of another noise, a thumping drumbeat. Was the earth rumbling again? What would they do if the whole landscape was on the Laird's side? Then she realised the noise was coming from above.

She peered up into the sky. All the swans of the estate were in the air again, flying in a wedge round the castle, their wings thrumming in time to the crashes and laughter from inside.

Pearl pulled her shoulders and spine away from the shuddering wall and looked at Emmie.

"So that's bloodlore," her little sister murmured. "Interesting."

"We should go now," said Pearl shakily. "Before the swans land again." Without even pausing to look into the ballroom, they ran the length of the castle wall.

The rhythm of boom and rattle behind them stilled for a moment and they heard a clear young voice screaming. Then silence. The girls paused by the corner of the castle, caught between the fight behind and the escape ahead.

"Was that Thomas?" asked Pearl. But she knew it was; she'd been arguing with that voice all morning. Had the scream been pain or triumph?

"Should we go back and help him?" Emmie asked.

Pearl looked over her shoulder. She thought of his long hand pulling her over the wall, and pulling her away from the swans. She remembered the same hand dangling her over the scree, and his silence when Emmie asked about the end of the ceremony.

"No," Pearl said firmly. "He chose this fight. We didn't. We must go and save Jasper and Ruby."

They dropped their pans on the grass and sprinted towards the canals, discussing the best way home.

"It'll be faster to go round by the river," panted Pearl.

"But it'll be safer through the mountains," said Emmie. "I'm pretty sure the Laird soaked the river path with blood, and that's how he got my horse to his land. Anyway, I haven't been in the mountains yet."

Pearl didn't really want to go through the Grey Men's Grave again, but it wouldn't be wise to follow a path sodden with bloodlore, even if it was a flatter, faster way home.

"Mountains then," she agreed, and they turned to the north.

As they ran, Emmie told Pearl about her morning. Pearl was amazed at her sister's cheerfulness. Perhaps Emmie hadn't understood just how dangerous the last few minutes had been. Perhaps she hadn't had such a good view of the dying rat.

Pearl tried to concentrate on her sister's story.

"When our rocking horses first came alive, it was fabulous fun. My white mare is much faster than the ponies in the stables, though those polished sides are harder to grip with your calves. She started off all happy, her tail flicking and her ears twitching. But once she'd left the other two horses, she started to sweat, at least I think it was sweat though it smelt like varnish. It was as if she was being forced to follow the path along the river, though I wasn't forcing her at all, I was just letting her have her head, but something was dragging her on. And when we reached the bridge into the Laird's lands, there he was, all smarmy smiles and fancy words, and my poor horse was terrified, and all those swans attacked her, and the Laird pretended to rescue me, though it was so obvious he'd set them on us in the first place. But I pretended to be grateful and a little bit stupid, and asked him to rescue my horse too, so we led her over those stinky canals and took her right inside that ridiculous castle, because he doesn't seem to care about mud and dust, does he? Then he gave me lemonade and cake and told me stories. The stories were fantastic, but the lemonade was sour and the cake was dry. Actually, I'm starving, do you have any food?"

"No. I fed it to the swans."

"Why did you do that?"

"To stop them biting chunks out of me and Thomas."

"Couldn't you have kept a little bit for me?"

"At least you've had cake, and Jasper's had blaeberries, and Ruby's got shortbread. I haven't eaten anything at all." Pearl tried to sound grumpy, but she was so relieved to have stolen Emmie back from the Laird and Thomas, and so proud of how her little sister had been flying rings round these oddly powerful people, that she couldn't hide her happiness. She laughed. "I'll eat like a horse when we get home!"

As they crossed the widest canal between the castle and the wall, the sunken grey swan stared up at them with one flat eye. Pearl glanced back at the castle and saw clouds of dust belching from its windows.

Were Thomas and the Laird still fighting in there? Was the winner going to come after them?

Pearl smiled at her sister, running beside her. Whoever won the duel in the castle, Pearl had already won the fight for Emmie.

But when they reached the base of the wall, Pearl's happiness crashed up against the stone barrier. "How will we get over?"

"Easy!" chirped Emmie. She flew to the top of the wall, twirled round and performed an exaggerated curtsey, holding the hem of her skirt.

"Super," growled Pearl. "But how do I get up?"

Emmie sat on the wall and offered Pearl her hand. Pearl stretched up. Their fingers didn't even touch.

Pearl looked round, but saw nothing on the grass she could stand on. And even if she could reach her sister's hand, Emmie's slim arm probably wouldn't hold her weight.

"I'm trapped," she said gloomily.

"No, you aren't." Emmie floated off the wall, hovered above Pearl's head, then sank down until their fingers touched. They clasped hands, but when Emmie pulled, Pearl's feet hardly left the ground. Emmie tried again, but she fell out of the air on top of Pearl. They lay in a heap beside a neat pile of sheep droppings, shaking with laughter.

After rolling her sister gently off, Pearl stood up and looked at the wall. She had managed to help Thomas to the top of it. She doubted she could ever lift Thomas's whole weight, but when he was leaping, she'd been able to give him a boost.

"Stay down here," she ordered Emmie, "and give me a shove when I jump."

Emmie kept her feet on the grass and got ready to boost Pearl up. But when Pearl leapt, Emmie didn't just shove, she launched herself into flight, so Pearl overshot, missed the top of the wall, and was thrown right over onto the rough ground on the other side.

"Ow! Be more careful!"

Emmie popped up over the wall, trying to hide a giggle. "Sorry. Are you alright?"

"No!" Pearl rubbed her bruised shoulder. "Thomas helped me over much more smoothly, even without flying."

"Ooooh! Thomas did, did he? Do you like him, then?"

"Like him? He's tried to kill me at least once!"

"Yes, but do you like him?"

"No. I don't. He's annoying. You're all annoying. I should just leave you alone to get on with your silly songs." She stomped off.

Then she turned back to Emmie. "If you can fly over a wall, why don't you just fly home? It would be quicker than going on foot with me, and you can rescue Ruby if I tell you where she is."

But Emmie was on the ground too, trudging along like Pearl.

"I could fly in the castle because I was borrowing the Laird's power. Getting us over that wall used up all the power I had left. I don't know how to store my own power properly yet. I suppose I need a stick, or a bone, or something. And I'll need to learn to take power and music straight from the land."

Emmie knelt down, laid her hand flat on the ground under some bracken and listened. Then she shook her head and began climbing again.

Pearl asked, "So how did you get from cakes and stories to flying round the ballroom?"

"Well, the Laird told me all these lovely tales about his family and the rocks and their music. Then a couple of crows flew in a broken window, and the Laird got all panicky and shouted at his swans and locked the doors. He said we should summon Ruby and Jasper to have a party, so he wanted me to sing with him. But I didn't believe him about the party, and I wouldn't join in. That's when he realised I wasn't all sugar and spice and all things silly, and he tried to grab me, but I grabbed some of his power and flew off. So he started to chase me, which was even more fun than galloping rocking horses. Then you arrived. So now it's your turn to tell me a story. Tell me how you found me."

As they climbed up to the Grey Men's Grave, Pearl told Emmie about finding Ruby and Jasper, and about crossing the mountains with Thomas. She told her little sister what Thomas had said about the rocking horses running from the swans and the triplets crowning his grandfather. But she couldn't find the words to tell Emmie that Thomas claimed his grandfather had created them.

Emmie asked Pearl to repeat Thomas's tale of the fight for the keystone, then said, "The Laird told me that story too, and that the keystone is the most powerful thing on this land. So I think we'd better go and find it."

"How would that help?" Pearl shook her head. "Are you hoping that if you gave it to the Earl or the Laird, they'd be so grateful they'd let you go home? But which family would you give it to? They're both as bad as each other."

"Give it to them? No, I don't think so. I might keep it for myself. Then I would have all the power the land could give me."

Emmie gave Pearl a beaming smile and kept going up the slope. Pearl followed, wondering if she had left Hansel inside the gingerbread house and rescued the witch instead.

Pearl's grazed skin stung as they clambered in a wide curve to avoid the scree and the cliff. When they reached the mouth of the Grey Men's Grave, it was in shadow again, the Keystone Peak now between the sun and the pass.

Emmie stared at the sharp summit of the Peak. "The keystone is up there."

"Perhaps," said Pearl. "Or perhaps it fell, or perhaps it never existed. Let's get going through the pass."

"No. Let's go and look for it."

"What?"

"Let's go and look for the keystone."

"Emmie! Is that why you wanted to come through the mountains? To get the keystone?"

Emmie looked up at her sister through her curls and smiled.

Pearl snapped, "How can you think of magical treasures from fairy tales when Ruby and Jasper are in danger? We have to rescue them before we do anything else. And it's not safe to climb the

Keystone Peak without climbing gear. Even our big brother never climbed it. We need to go home. Now."

"You go home if you like, Pearl, but I think the best way to stay safe in a war between the Swanns and the Horsburghs is to hold the only thing more powerful than they are. So I'm climbing the Keystone Peak."

The sisters stood at the edge of the cliff and glared at each other.

Emmie had the blonde curls, pink cheeks and wide eyes of all the triplets, but when she closed off the smile, Pearl recognised her own square chin.

Pearl clenched her fists and shoved them in her pockets. "I'm your big sister. I came all this way to save you. You have to do what I say!"

Emmie put her hands on her hips. "I was doing fine on my own, thanks. And what I *have* to do is find the keystone."

Pearl remembered Ruby sniffling and Jasper gazing at Thomas, and she yelled, "Not one of you pays any attention to me! I don't know why I'm bothering to rescue you! You're simply not worth it!"

As Pearl turned away in disgust, she saw, far below, the tiny figures of a horse and rider galloping from the castle towards the mountains.

"Thomas! He's coming after us!"

Emmie looked down. "He's riding my horse! How dare he!"

"Surely he won't risk jumping the horse over that wall."

But Thomas leapt off the toy horse, twisted his

staff, and blasted a hole in the wall with a deep clang which they heard echoing from the slopes around.

Pearl frowned at this fast and destructive way of dealing with the barrier. Maybe Thomas hadn't needed her boost over the wall at all. Perhaps the oath, the handclasp and the thank you had just been a way to get Pearl on his side again. She sighed, remembering how she'd helped him break into the castle then led him to Emmie. She'd made it too easy for him.

Thomas gave quick instructions to the white horse, who trotted off towards the river. Then he began climbing, digging his precious staff viciously into the sparse undergrowth to haul himself up as fast as he could.

"He's in a bad mood," said Emmie. "And we have nothing to defend ourselves with. We have to get the keystone."

She turned her back on the boy below and headed for the steeper slope of the Keystone Peak.

Pearl sighed and followed her little sister. She had always wanted to conquer this mountain, and it was a beautiful day for a climb.

Chapter 18

Pearl and Emmie had a lot less breath to chat or argue; they were pushing up an ever steeper slope as fast as their legs could bear.

Even so, Pearl found enough breath to ask, "What does this keystone *do*?"

"From what Thomas told you, and what the Laird told me, I think it links people who can hear the land to the music and power of these mountains."

"What does it look like?"

"I've no idea," said Emmie cheerfully. "I'll listen when we get there. I'm sure I'll find it."

Pearl had been just as confident she could find Emmie in a silent castle, so it was hard to challenge this vague optimism. Instead she climbed even faster, got ahead of her sister, and concentrated on finding the best way up.

She checked behind and below occasionally, but she couldn't see Thomas. The lower slopes were hidden from this height; he could be following them, even catching up.

Would he know where they were going? He wasn't a skilled tracker, but he might have seen them turn away from the pass and begin to climb the Keystone Peak.

There was no point in worrying about Thomas, Pearl decided. Emmie was determined to reach the summit whether he was following them or not.

They strode round scattered heaps of boulders, the dour grey piles brightened by thin stripes of white quartzite or small lumps of pink granite.

The ascent of the peak was no more difficult, so far, than any of the mountains in the northern range. "I *can* do this on my own," Pearl murmured, "without Father by my side or Peter's maps in my head."

Pearl led Emmie over a lip at the top of the slope, onto the plateau with the jutting peak on its western edge.

The plateau was formed from flat plates of grey stone, lying beside each other like tiles. However, the rocks weren't level, nor were they fitted neatly together. They were tilted and skewed, as if an ancient mosaic's smooth pattern had been distorted when the floor underneath subsided.

The slabs didn't wobble as the girls put their weight on them, but Pearl saw hollow dark space between them as she stepped over the cracks, and wondered how stable they were. She wondered what happened to mountains when they sang. Was it safe to walk on them?

"I can't go any further, Pearl, I have to sit down." Emmie flopped onto a grey slab. Pearl knelt down to rub her little sister's leg muscles so they didn't seize up.

"Stretch out," she said. "Just for five minutes. If Thomas has worked out where we're going, we need to stay well ahead of him." Emmie lay down on the flat rock.

Pearl saw a sudden spark of colour by Emmie's head. She scrambled forward. In the gap between the slabs, flowers were growing: tiny alpine plants with short thick stems, small dark leaves and pinprick bright flowers. The only plants she'd seen thriving on the whole mountain range. In this one little dip, there were four different colours.

"Look, Emmie!" she said in delight. "It's the narrowest flowerbed I've ever seen."

Emmie rolled over and peered in. "How can they grow so high up?"

"They're sheltered from the wind, the rain runs off the slabs to water them and the rock holds the heat of the sun. It's a mountain greenhouse. Perhaps these mountains aren't finished yet."

Emmie lay back down. "A greenhouse? Are there any tomatoes growing there? Any bananas or pineapples?"

"Are you really hungry?"

"Famished. Are you sure you don't have any snacks in your pockets? That pinafore's usually better than a picnic basket."

"All I had was a carrot, which I fed to Conker, and a sandwich, which I fed to the swans."

"Please look again, Pearl. I'm starving."

So Pearl emptied her pockets. She pulled out an empty matchbox, scraps of paper, chewed pencil stubs, half a ruler, a tartan ribbon, a hoofpick and three different thicknesses of string.

Pearl frowned at the crushed matchbox and the splintered ruler, and felt the bruises from the scree ache all over her body. What else had the rocks broken? She pulled out sharp fragments of stripy snail shells and a blue speckled feather now snapped in two.

Emmie was rummaging through the pile.

"You can't eat any of that," Pearl pointed out.

"I know, but there might be something useful."

"It can *all* be useful," said Pearl, "depending on what you need at the time."

She added to the pile. A couple of rocks from the riverbank, handkerchiefs, a reed she'd been making into a whistle, the oilcloth which had protected the mirror and a few fingerfuls of fluff.

"That's it." She patted the pinafore. "My pockets are empty. No food at all. We'd better get going." She started to fill her pockets again.

"What's this?" Emmie untangled a jagged stone from a lacy handkerchief. It was dark grey and shiny, reflecting light from its many irregular surfaces.

Pearl glanced at the stone as she wound the ribbon neatly round her fingers. "I think it's a flint, so I tried to chip it into an arrowhead. But it's not very sharp."

The stone was shaped like a beech leaf, with a blunt point at one end, then it curved outwards and back to a sharper point. The tiny hollows and planes formed by Pearl's careful chipping made it look like a large smoky gem, cut for a giant's ring.

"It's lovely," said Emmie. "It's as old as the mountains, but you've made it new. It might be useful, but I don't think it would bring down a deer." She handed it back, and watched as Pearl put it in a pocket.

Pearl stood up, stretched and turned towards to

the summit of the Keystone Peak. Emmie stood up too. She groaned.

"We don't have to climb all the way to the top," Pearl said gently.

"Yes, we do." Emmie pointed back the way they had come.

Thomas was clambering onto the plateau.

Pearl seized Emmie's hand and they ran, away from Thomas and towards the summit.

They were startled by a crash from behind them. Both girls turned to see Thomas strike his staff on a rock and produce another echoing boom.

"Emerald Chayne. I defeated the Laird for you. Now I've come to lead you to your destiny. Don't let your sister take you home to be bored and respectable. Come with me and enjoy your true power."

Emmie's voice carried through the clear mountain air. "My destiny is ahead of me, not behind. And it isn't with you and your grandfather."

She hauled on Pearl's hand and they raced over the uneven tiles. Thomas's voice followed them. "If you come with me now, I won't harm either of you. But if you defy me, Emmie, I will sweep your sister out of the way to get at you. Do you want to see her fly, like the Grey Men flew?"

Emmie looked up at Pearl, her face filled with doubt for the first time that afternoon.

Chapter 19

Pearl looked around quickly. Unless she wanted to jump off the mountain, there were only two ways off the plateau: west, up to the summit; or east, down to the Grey Men's Grave. Thomas blocked the eastern descent, and Emmie's keystone, if it existed, might be at the top of the western ascent. So Pearl grinned reassuringly at her sister. "Don't worry about me. He's just a big bully. Let's get your stone."

She let go of Emmie's hand so they wouldn't pull each other off balance as they jumped from slab to slab. Then she led the way swiftly across the narrowing plain of flat rocks, towards the sharp ridge rising to the summit.

The boom Thomas had used to get their attention sounded again, but now Pearl felt the distant noise as well as heard it. He was hurling the same crashing power at them as he'd used to wreck the castle.

Pearl pushed Emmie in front of her, getting between her sister and the next wave of sound. A blast hit Pearl's shoulder, knocking her down to her knees. She scrambled to her feet and kept running, bruises throbbing.

But it was hard to keep moving fast across

the tilted tiles while bracing herself for the next painful blow. When she looked back to see when it would come, she saw Thomas sprinting towards them. His next bolt of power would hit her even harder because he'd be much closer.

As he raised his staff, Pearl turned to face him. "Keep going, Emmie. I'll try to stop him."

"Don't be daft. What will you stop him with?"

As Thomas twisted his staff, Emmie slipped in front of Pearl and spread her arms wide.

When the sound reached them, Emmie didn't flinch from it or grunt with the impact; she curled her arms round the wave of air and seemed to embrace it. Pearl watched in amazement as Thomas sent another boom, and Emmie caught that too.

Thomas lowered his staff and frowned.

"This is easy," Emmie said. "Perhaps he's not as clever as he looks. But I wish I had somewhere sensible to store this power. Let's keep going, Pearl, but if you think he's going to send another blast, tell me. I want as much of his power as I can hold."

Pearl and Emmie ran towards the ridge, trying to ignore their tiring legs, checking constantly behind them. Every time Thomas stopped and aimed the staff at them, Emmie faced him with her arms wide.

Thomas must have realised that his sound blasts were no longer harming them, that Emmie even welcomed them, because he stopped attacking and just kept chasing them.

When they were only a hundred yards from

the start of the ridge, Pearl turned again and saw that Thomas was no longer running. He lifted his staff, planted it in the space between two slabs, and knelt down beside it. Pearl saw his hand curl round the staff, and remembered the rock that had moved in the Grey Men's Grave.

She called to Emmie, "Faster! I think he's trying to move the stones."

Emmie leapt from slab to slab. "This is like the game where bears eat you if you stand on the cracks in the pavement!"

Pearl grunted. "But in Perth the bears are pretend." She glanced back at the real threat behind them, and saw a ripple of rock start at Thomas's staff. It moved towards them like a wave. The slabs flicked up and down, like checked squares on a tablecloth being shaken free of crumbs.

"Run, Emmie!"

Pearl glanced back as they ran, and saw the rocks in front of Thomas lift high and crash down. For a heartbeat, she worried about the flowers in between them. Then she concentrated on getting as far away from Thomas as fast as she could.

A moment later, she heard the slabs right behind her shift.

"Keep running, Emmie!"

The stone beneath her boots twisted and she slid backwards. She saw the gaps between the slabs widening, and wondered what the inside of a mountain looked like. Then the rocks ahead rose and fell, like a churning sea of stone, and Emmie was tossed in the air. They reached for each other's hands and Pearl hauled Emmie onto her rocking stone.

The motion swung them round to face Thomas, crouched on the shore of the bucking slabs, shaking with effort, gripping his staff and singing a deep moaning command. Higher and faster waves spread out towards the girls.

Emmie stood in front of Pearl. "Hold me steady, but leave my hands free."

So Pearl, struggling to keep her own balance, wrapped her arms round her sister's waist.

Emmie held out her hands, palms down, fingers spread, and she sang. Her notes were pure and strong, her words calm and soothing, her voice clear and convincing, as if she was singing in her mother tongue. Pearl felt her sister's body shudder against her ribcage as Emmie pushed all the energy she could onto the rock beneath their feet.

The rocking slab slowed, steadied and stopped. It held them still and safe, while the rest of the slabs on the plateau slipped and crashed.

"How did you learn to do that?" Pearl still held her sister tight.

"I didn't! I'm just making it up."

"Can you make us a path of stepping stones up to the ridge?"

"No, I've used all the power I took from Thomas holding this one." Emmie's hands dropped to her sides.

Thomas lifted his head and looked at them, together on one small calm island in a sea of chaos.

Emmie waved at him, wiggling the tips of her fingers.

Thomas waved back. "Well done, Emerald!" he called. "You must have a rare skill to seize and use energy like that. I can't store any power without my staff. And how clever of you to use *all* that stolen energy to hold your stone steady. But now you haven't got any power left! What a shame!"

Emmie sagged in Pearl's arms. "Oh no. We've done exactly what he wanted. He wanted me to use up the power he gave me. Sorry."

"Maybe he *is* as clever as he looks," muttered Pearl. Then she shouted, "I thought you weren't like the Laird, Thomas. I thought you never forced the land to move for you. I thought you wanted to heal it not hurt it!"

Thomas looked down at the moving stones, then back up at the girls. "Wars aren't won by sticking to the rules. And you two aren't doing *anything* the way we expected. The triplets weren't meant to run or hide or argue or fight. You're meant to be on *our* side! You're making this day very difficult, so I think I'm justified in doing anything to get you back." He grinned suddenly. "And if you don't agree, Pearl, if you want to make me feel guilty, then you just stay right there and I'll come and discuss it with you!"

He stood up, pulled his staff from the ground, and started running towards them. As soon as he lifted the staff, the slabs ahead of him began to settle down, but jolting and jerking stones still surrounded Emmie and Pearl.

"We can't wait for them all to stop moving; he'll reach us before then," decided Pearl. "Run for the summit!"

So Pearl and Emmie turned, jumped onto the shifting rock behind them and tried to run over the lurching plateau.

The stones slid apart, leaving deep gaps under their feet; the stones crashed together, threatening to crush them between edges and corners. Pearl leapt off each slab not knowing if it would follow her upwards, knocking her feet from under her; she aimed for the next slab not knowing if it would still be there when she landed.

She kept one stone behind Emmie, and watched as her sister, with shorter legs but more grace, timed her leaps well. Soon the slabs were moving less violently, but Pearl knew that if the last ripple was reaching them, so was Thomas.

She looked round. He was much closer now, moving fast on stones that lay flat just as he reached them, and she could see exhilaration on his face. He was getting to fight his war today.

The girls had almost reached the edge of the plateau. The start of the ridge reared up ahead of them.

"Emmie," Thomas yelled, "Emmie. I still have years' worth of power in my staff, but you've used up your stolen power and you've no lore to help you gather more. You've nothing left to fight me with."

The girls leapt off the last shuddering slab onto the sharp ridge.

"I don't want to hurt you, Emmie, because I need to take you to my grandfather. But I don't need Pearl. And you have no power left to protect her. Come back here, Emmie!"

Emmie called, "I won't turn back now. And I won't let you hurt my sister." She nodded at Pearl. "Lead on, big sister. I'll be right behind you."

So Pearl started up the ridge to the summit, her little sister a step behind, a shield between her and Thomas.

The ridge hung like a silver shawl on a clothes line, pegged to the corner of the plateau at one end and to the summit of the Keystone at the other; sweeping up in a line to the peak, draping down either side. The ridge was so narrow, Pearl expected it to sway and billow in a breath of wind.

Even if Emmie hadn't been protecting Pearl's back, they couldn't have climbed two abreast, and it was impossible to run. They had to walk carefully, watching their footing with every step. Pearl hoped Thomas would be walking just as slowly; if he moved less cautiously, he could catch up before they reached the summit.

There was no safe path along the ridge. Pearl was climbing along the slanted top edge of layered rock, jamming her feet into corners, using the angle of the rock to stop herself slipping.

"If he makes these rocks move, we'll have no chance. It's dangerous enough with everything standing still."

"He can't dislodge you without dislodging me too," murmured Emmie. "We just have to reach the top and get the keystone before he does."

Pearl looked at the pointed peak ahead. There was nothing there but bare rock. There was nothing under her feet but bare rock. There was nothing around her but air.

She heard breathing behind her. Emmie's shallow fast breathing. Was that Thomas's breathing too, harder, deeper, catching up?

Pearl concentrated on each step, each breath.

Left, right, left, right. In, out, in, out.

She waited fearfully for a punch of sound between her shoulders, or for the stone under her boots to shift and fall.

Left, right; in, out.

She kept going, racing at a snail's pace to the summit.

Chapter 20

Pearl placed each foot carefully, arms out for balance, moving along the ridge only slightly faster than she would walk along a garden wall.

"Hurry!" said Emmie behind her. "Hurry! Thomas is catching up. If he gets really close he can aim round me and reach you."

Pearl glanced back briefly. Thomas was moving with care, but with his eyes on Emmie, not on his feet. He was no more than sixty yards behind them. She looked ahead at the summit. It was about forty yards ahead.

Then she heard a clatter and a gasp.

Emmie had slipped and fallen awkwardly, with one leg bent under her and her hands splayed out, grasping the edge of the ridge. As Pearl bent down to grab Emmie, a wave of sound slid above her, rippling her hair.

Pearl pulled Emmie back up between herself and Thomas. He lowered his staff. "Nearly!" he yelled. "Give up now, girls, and we can all get down safely."

"Are you alright?" asked Pearl.

Emmie nodded. "Just keep going."

They set off again. With Thomas still further behind them than their goal was in front of them,

Pearl thought they could reach the summit before he caught up.

The race to the top was the one race against Thomas she could win today.

But Pearl suddenly realised it was a pointless race to win: when they reached the summit, they would be exposed, with nowhere to hide or run from Thomas's anger and power. Losing this race would still be a victory for Thomas, because he would have them trapped at the finishing line.

Unless they won the prize as well as the race. Unless they found the keystone, a treasure from a bedtime story which even the story's heroes had never seen.

"What exactly are we looking for on the summit?" Pearl croaked at Emmie, almost choking with effort and fear.

"The keystone, of course."

"But what will it look like?"

"I don't know," Emmie admitted. "I'm just hoping it will be obvious when we get there."

"Couldn't we just pick up any old stone, wave it at Thomas and see if it frightens him?"

"Does he seem easily frightened to you?"

Pearl was balancing too carefully to shake her head.

The ridge widened slightly as it tipped up towards the summit. They didn't dare climb it side by side as it would give Thomas a clear shot at Pearl's back. But with the safety of a few paces of rock on either side, Pearl broke into a run, pushing herself as hard as she could. Emmie stayed just one step behind.

Suddenly Pearl reached the top. What looked like a sharp peak from a distance was as level on top as a billiard table, and twice as wide. But the true summit was at the northern edge, a point of rock higher than the rest by the height of Emmie's shoulders.

"Hunt for the keystone!" ordered Pearl, walking swiftly to the centre of the mountaintop. Was it a building block? A crystal? Was it carved by hand or shaped by the weather? She kicked in panic at the few boring lumps of rock scattered around.

"Emmie!" she called urgently. Emmie wasn't looking for anything. She was standing with her hand on the true summit of the Keystone Peak.

"Pearl," Emmie said calmly, "please give me the flint from your pocket."

Pearl put her hand in her pocket.

Thomas stepped onto the summit.

Pearl stretched out her arm and gave the arrowhead to Emmie, who held it in her right hand and grasped Pearl's hand with her left.

"Don't let go of me," Emmie whispered.

Thomas walked towards them. "Were you searching for the keystone? Haven't you found it? Bad luck, girls."

He lifted his staff. "Pearl. I'm sorry you never heard the music of the land."

He pointed his staff straight at her and smiled. Not a glittering smile, nor a charming smile, nor a wolfish smile. Just a slightly squint smile that actually wrinkled his eyes, and may even have been regret. "I am sorry, Pearl."

Pearl gripped her sister's hand tightly, and gulped a breath of cold air.

"Don't worry," Emmie said confidently. "She'll hear this."

Emmie struck the true summit with the flint.

It rang like a bell. A bell the size of a mountain.

The whole mountain shook, vibrating and resonating. Pearl held onto Emmie, and Emmie held onto the flint. They moved with the sound, held safe within its waves.

So the keystone rang, and Pearl heard the land sing.

Thomas was rocked off his feet and thrown into the air. He fell backwards and out of Pearl's sight, flying off the Keystone Peak, just like his grey-haired ancestor.

As the Keystone Peak vibrated, it was joined by the weaker off-key notes of the other mountains in the range. They sang with one voice, as Pearl and Emmie stood surrounded by the pulse of the rocks.

Pearl waited impatiently for the noise to stop. When the summit stilled, she rushed to the edge to look for Thomas, who was far too young to go grey into a grave.

He lay sprawled at the top of the ridge, where it widened out, looking clumsy for the first time since she'd met him. His staff was lying abandoned by his open fingers. His hair was black. But he wasn't moving.

Pearl scrambled down to him, put her hand on his cheek and watched his chest. He was still breathing.

Emmie walked down to them.

"That explains why no one ever took the keystone off the mountain. It *is* the mountain," said Emmie.

"Could you pop this back in your pinafore? I don't have pockets in this dress." She handed the flint to Pearl, then she looked at Thomas. "Is he alive?"

"Yes, but he's unconscious."

"What was he going to do?"

"Kill me and take you."

They looked at him silently.

Finally, Emmie asked, "What should we do with him?"

Pearl said quietly, "Perhaps it's his destiny to die here." She raised her eyebrows at her newly powerful little sister, wondering how Emmie would choose to use her strength and ambition.

Emmie pursed her lips and thought for a moment. "We have to help him."

Pearl sighed with relief. "Of course we do."

She turned back to Thomas and brushed the hair off his forehead.

His eyes opened.

Pearl moved faster than either her sister or Thomas, and pulled the staff away from his outstretched hand.

Emmie said in a sharp sweet voice, "I'll take that. You help him up."

"No!" Pearl stepped away from them both.

Thomas spoke hoarsely, "Please give me the staff. I need it to help me stand."

"No!" repeated Pearl. "I'll keep it, so we can get off this mountain without any loud noises or moving rocks."

Thomas sat up and glared at her. Emmie put her hands on her hips and pouted.

Pearl held the heavy stick tightly. It pressed

uncomfortably against her pinafore, forcing the blunt point of the flint into her leg.

Thomas stood up and dusted his trousers down. "Please give me my staff, Pearl. I do admit that you've defeated me, for now, but I can't be without my staff."

"No. It's too dangerous in your hands, in the hands of anyone who thinks they have a right to power." She glanced at her sister, then back to Thomas. "If you try to take it from me, I will drop it." She dangled the staff over the edge of the ridge.

Thomas held his hands up in a gesture of acceptance, but his eyes were dark and angry.

"Now, Thomas, are you hurt?" Pearl asked, feeling more in control. "Can you walk?"

He rolled his shoulders and flexed his fingers. "I'm fine." He took a long step towards her. "See?"

"Stay back!" ordered Pearl.

Thomas scowled. Pearl waved the staff over the edge again. Emmie giggled.

Thomas opened his mouth, but Pearl never found out if he was going to agree or argue, because his words were drowned out by the huge hooting of a horn. Like a hunting horn, but louder than thunder, and more exhilarating than a whole pipe band.

When the horn's halloo ended, the joyful noise echoed round the mountains. Then Pearl heard more than an echo. A couple of high notes flew around their heads, chirruping and dancing, as if they were chasing the music of the horn.

Thomas stood taller, his angry face smoothed into a smile.

Emmie turned pale.

"What? What?" Pearl looked at the two of them. Something had changed, but she didn't know what. She still held the staff, but she seemed to have lost control.

"That was my grandfather," Thomas said proudly. "He's come to hunt the Laird. But who has he brought with him? You know, don't you, Emmie? You recognised their voices, didn't you?"

"Jasper and Ruby," Emmie whispered. "That was Jasper and Ruby."

Chapter 21

"Jasper *and* Ruby?" repeated Pearl. "How did he get Ruby?" She turned on Thomas. "How did your grandfather get Ruby?"

He grinned at her. "You know I didn't bring you into the mountains just for the pleasure of your company, Pearl. I did hope you would tell me where Ruby was, but I wasn't sure I could persuade you."

"Or force me." She glared at him.

"Indeed. So in the note Jasper took to Horsburgh Hall, I told my grandfather you'd probably hidden Ruby in the wood, because you hadn't had time to take her home. I suggested Grandfather use Jasper as bait to lure her out. Why didn't you tell her to stay hidden? Why didn't you arrange a password?"

"I told her not to come out for anyone but me." Pearl's tired shoulders slumped, and the tip of the staff scraped on the rock. "But she doesn't usually do what I tell her."

Thomas smirked. "This changes everything. I've won now, haven't I, Pearl? I have two triplets, and you only have one. So give me back my staff, and we'll go safely and quietly down the hill, as you so sensibly suggest. Then Emmie and I will meet my grandfather and find her destiny. Pearl, my dear, you can go home for tea, or come and argue against fate. It's up to you."

He held out his hand for the staff.

Pearl tightened her fist round the stick.

"Fine." Thomas shrugged. "You carry it if you like. It's long and heavy and awkward, and you can't make it work, and you'll have to give it back eventually. But you keep pretending you're in charge if you really want to."

Pearl looked at Emmie, who said in a small voice, "He's right. He has won. I have to go with him, so I can join Ruby and Jasper. At least we tried, Pearl, we tried our best, but the Earl and Thomas are stronger than us, and we'll just have to do what they want." She sniffed.

Pearl stared at her sister. Had she given up? Emmie sniffed again. Pearl dropped the staff on the ground. It clattered like a dead branch. She turned to walk down the mountain.

Then she looked back to see if her sister had been pretending and was about to ambush Thomas, but Emmie was standing passively as he waved his staff over her head and down her sides.

"Just checking that you don't have lots of power stored somewhere, Emmie," he explained. "You created an amazingly strong connection with the mountains for a moment, even without the lost keystone."

Emmie glanced over at Pearl, and shook her head very slightly.

Thomas kept talking. "Your skills are even more unusual than your brother's. But you don't know how to use them yet, so I don't want you carrying lots of power around, not before the ceremony."

"I don't have anywhere to store power yet," Emmie said calmly. "Where did you get your staff?"

Pearl tried to stomp off in a huff, but that wasn't safe on the narrow ridge, so she just walked on steadily. Emmie and Thomas followed, having a remarkably friendly conversation about the right way to store the power of the land. Pearl couldn't move fast enough to escape from their cheerful voices.

"It's called a lorefast," Thomas explained. "Everyone who knows landlore needs one to store the power of the land's music. The Laird has a bone because he still uses bloodlore. I have a staff from an old rowan tree. My grandfather has a bull's horn."

"Can you inherit them, or do you need to find your own?" Emmie asked.

"Everyone needs their own fresh lorefast to master the lore, but the ancient lorefasts are the strongest. The lorefast of the last Lord of Landlaw Hold stores centuries of power, and it's been passed down in my family. But you have to earn the right to use the ancient lorefasts."

Pearl forgot she was trying to ignore them and turned carefully round. "That's what the Laird meant. That's why you're trying so hard to crown your grandfather. You want to earn the old lorefast."

"Aren't you clever, Pearl? Yes, if I deliver all the triplets and the Laird to my grandfather, he's promised me the lorefast of Landlaw Hold. Then I will have all the power my family has ever gathered. My grandfather's only interested in these small hills, but I want to use my landlore everywhere."

He kept Emmie moving in front of him with a gentle hand on her shoulder. "So that's how your destiny is bound up with mine, Emmie. You'll crown my grandfather, and I'll gain more power than he has ever handled."

"I would like a lorefast too," Emmie said in a chirpy voice. "If I could find a new one, not an ancient one like the one you want, would you teach me to use it? You'd be an inspiring teacher."

"You'd be an interesting pupil. We could do a lot together. But ... we'll see." His face hardened. "Come on," he snapped at Pearl. "Hurry up. We must get all the triplets together."

So Pearl led the way down the mountain.

The ridge didn't seem so dangerous now. The weather was sunny and windless, the rocky path seemed wider than it had a few minutes ago. The way down is never as exciting as the way up, and she wasn't being chased any more, so Pearl had plenty of time to think.

When she glanced behind, Emmie was looking as cheerful as a child going to a picnic, and Thomas was looking triumphant.

But Pearl felt miserable. Yet again, she had nearly rescued a triplet; yet again, she had ended up doing exactly what Thomas wanted.

What else could she have done? She had hidden Ruby and told her little sister to stay in the hut until she returned, but Ruby must have opened the door for Jasper and the Earl. She had rescued

Jasper, but he had bitten and betrayed her. She and Emmie had knocked Thomas off the summit and disarmed him, but now they were being herded tamely towards his grandfather.

As they reached the foot of the ridge, Pearl heard Emmie ask Thomas politely how he'd moved the heavy plateau stones. Pearl shook her head. Didn't Emmie remember that Thomas had nearly killed them both here?

Pearl jumped off the ridge onto the squint slabs of the plateau. This violent landscape hadn't been created by geological forces many millennia ago, but by an arrogant ambitious boy just an hour ago.

She knelt down and searched the gaps between the nearest slabs. The pale roots of a small plant pointed up to the sky. There were no flowers left.

Thomas and Emmie stepped onto the slab.

"You killed the flowers!" accused Pearl. "You destroyed everything when you forced the land to move, just to trick Emmie into using up her power. If you really loved the land, rather than the power it gives you, you would never treat it like this."

To Pearl's surprise, Thomas knelt beside her, and looked urgently around at the crushed plants and tumbled rock.

Then he shouted, "Here! Here are some that survived!"

All three heads bent over the dark gap between two slabs. In the warm shelter was a tiny plant with half a dozen bright blue trumpet-shaped flowers. A sudden smile swept round all three faces.

"See! I didn't destroy it, I just shook it up a bit." Thomas patted the stone. "The whole plateau will be blooming by next year. Especially once the crowning ceremony allows us to sing with the mountains properly again."

He leapt up, filled with new confidence. "Come on."

Pearl and Emmie stood and watched as he moved over the land, crossing whole slabs with every stride.

Pearl whispered, "I'm trying to think of an escape plan ..."

Thomas whirled round. "Come with me, Emmie." He held out a hand. "You can go your own way, Pearl, or you can come and see your brother and sister again."

Emmie walked towards Thomas, but looked back at Pearl. "Please come, Pearl. I'd like you to see my destiny. Will you come with us?"

Pearl couldn't understand why Emmie was being so co-operative, but she nodded reluctantly.

She trailed behind, her pockets heavy and her legs tired, snorting as she listened to Emmie chattering to Thomas about landlore. He was twisting his hands and staff, growing more extravagant every time Emmie said "Oh how fascinating!" and "Gosh, really?" and "My goodness, aren't you clever!"

Thomas might believe he'd beaten Pearl already, but he still needed all three triplets together to crown the Earl. If she could get Emmie away, the Horsburghs couldn't complete their crowning. If she could get Emmie really far away — to Perth or Edinburgh or London or Paris — then Thomas could never crown his grandfather and Pearl would have time to rescue the others.

They reached the edge of the plateau. Through the clear air, they could see the Grey Men's Grave below and the Anvil opposite; the river to the south and the moors to the north; and far to the north and west, the silky smudges of even higher mountains on the horizon.

Thomas lifted his hands high above his head. "All these mountains were created by movement deep under the earth's crust, which thrust layers of rock over each other into great folds and ridges." His hands sank down again. "Now they're being worn away."

Emmie gazed at him. "Really! How amazing."

Pearl stared at her sister. Emmie always got top marks in geology. She knew all about mountain uplift and erosion. Why was she playing daft like this?

"So the land is used to movement." Thomas scuffed his boot on a slab. "Pearl's angry that I shook the plateau, and she's right to accuse me of breaking my own rules, but I will heal any damage as soon as we're linked to the mountains again. Anyway, I haven't wrecked it forever, because all land is used to change: change by earthquakes, by volcanoes, by ice ages. By man too."

"Which man?" chirruped Emmie.

Thomas laughed. "All of us. The deer forests, grouse moors and pheasant woods of our land are as man-made as the fields and cities further south."

He crouched down and picked up a fragment of jagged rock. It was plain grey at first glance, but when Thomas twisted it in the sunlight it glittered with pink and white and black crystals.

"When the land is shaped by hot rocks shifting deep in the earth, it has a pulse and a rhythm, it has its own music. When it's exposed on the cold surface, the memory of that rhythm keeps the land supple so it can adapt to change. Weather and time; shifts in temperature and sea level; man's farms and factories: these can become part of the landscape, rather than destroy it.

"But if no one listens to the land, if no one stores and shares the rhythms, then the land forgets its music, forgets the movement. It becomes brittle, it fractures rather than flows under pressure, and it's worn away too easily by ice or rain or wind.

"For the land, movement is life. For the land, erosion is death."

He stood up again. "These mountains are silent because our ancestors lost the keystone, and forgot how to sing to them, so these peaks are crumbling faster than normal. If I don't win, they'll become scree ..." he glanced at Pearl, "... scree and pebbles, sand and clay. Then there will be nothing here but a flat gritty desert."

"A desert? In Scotland?" Pearl laughed uncomfortably. She'd finally found a statement of his which she could challenge. "It would be a very cold wet desert."

"Cold but not wet," said Thomas. "Without the mountains, there'd be less rain. They reach to the clouds and pull down the water which wears them away. But if we can link to the mountains' music again, it'll take much longer to wear them down."

Pearl was determined not to crumble under Thomas's contradictory weapons of strong science and convenient nonsense. But before she could challenge him again, Thomas and Emmie strode off down the heathery slope below the plateau. Pearl trudged after them, wondering how to stop this boy and his dangerous plans for the triplets.

She had no magic, no lore, no fancy powers. But she was walking behind her enemy on a mountain, and anyone can harness gravity. She speeded up to get closer.

Emmie was asking, "So, Thomas, does all the land in the world need songs?"

"Once, every piece of land had its own songs, sung by its own families. In most places, the families still sing quietly, the land prospers and no one notices. But a few families have left or died out, and some land has been forgotten or fought over. That silent land is eroding faster, just like our mountains. But even long neglected land still holds a few echoes, like you found on the Keystone Peak, and I think I could hear those echoes and help that land.

"Most landlore families can only hear their home, the land they're connected to, but I can hear more. I've sung with the grounds round my school, because I spend half the year there. So, with a stronger lorefast, I think I could sing with any land that has been abandoned and forgotten."

"How wonderful!" Emmie said enthusiastically. "And of course, once the land is singing again, you'll find other people who can hear the land to share it with, won't you?"

Thomas stopped, and Pearl stopped too. She needed to stay behind him.

Thomas stared at Emmie. "What do you mean?"

Emmie smiled innocently. "Don't you think it would be fairer? Surely people would love their land best if they only had a small piece each?"

"You think I should do all the work: babysitting the three of you, fighting off protective big sisters, learning my landlore, earning my lorefast, practising skills day and night for years, building up my strength and power, waking and nurturing and loving the land, then give it away? Just give it away?"

"Oh, I'm sure you know best. I was just wondering ..." Emmie shrugged and walked on, followed by Thomas, then Pearl.

Pearl was wondering too. What was her sister doing? Perhaps she wasn't being quite as co-operative as she seemed. Perhaps she did have a plan.

But Pearl had a plan too, and she had to act soon or lose her chance forever.

They were leaving the plateau at an angle, heading towards a corrie which led straight down to the Laird's land, avoiding the Grey Men's Grave. The corrie was a steep bowl of space scooped out of the side of the Keystone Peak: the most direct way down, but not the easiest. As they arrived at the highest point of the corrie, Thomas stopped and looked around.

"My grandfather has wanted to hear these mountains all his life. But I want," he swept his arms out to pull in the entire landscape, "I want to hear the whole island, the whole planet."

Thomas balanced elegantly on the top edge

of the corrie, looking not at his feet, nor at his audience, but at the world he wanted to conquer.

Pearl focused on a spot between his shoulder blades and flung herself forward.

Before she could collide with Thomas to send one or both of them over the edge, she was knocked sideways and landed with a mouth full of heather at Thomas's heels.

Thomas stepped neatly out of the way, as Pearl twisted round to stare up at his rescuer, now sitting heavily on her chest.

Emmie.

"Why did you do that?" the girls shouted at each other.

Emmie put her face close to Pearl's, and their voices dropped.

"What are you trying to do?" Emmie whispered.

"I'm trying to save you," Pearl croaked back. "I don't know why I keep trying. Whenever I get you away from him, you all just trot right back like puppies. Do you really want to be with that poisonous boy?"

"Yes!"

"Yes?"

"Yes! He will teach me so much if I ask the right questions, and he's leading us to Ruby and Jasper. We have to stay with him."

Pearl shook her head. "If he gets all of you together, they'll force you into this crowning rite. If we keep you apart, they can't use you."

"If the three of us are so powerful together, perhaps it isn't just the Horsburghs who can use our power." Emmie leant closer. "Trust me, Pearl."

"Be careful. He's more dangerous than he looks."

"I know that," replied Emmie. "But so am I."

Emmie rolled off and let Pearl sit up. "Did anything fall out of your pockets when you landed?"

Pearl patted her pinafore. "No, I don't think so."

"Good. Come on, and listen to what he says; you might learn something."

Thomas grinned as the girls stood up and brushed dried heather from their skirts. "Don't you like your little sister chatting to me, Pearl? Are you still trying to get her home for tea?"

Red-faced, Pearl muttered, "We're going to need to eat eventually."

Thomas laughed. "Are you hungry? Is that why you're so grumpy?" From his slim waistcoat pocket he pulled a paper packet of mintcake, the food climbers and explorers carried to give them energy.

Pearl, Emmie and Thomas stood together, the world glowing at their feet, the sweet mintcake dissolving in their mouths, the sun warming their tired shoulders. Pearl wondered how such a gorgeous day could be so threatening and strange.

Then Emmie wiped her mouth on her sleeve and said, "Let's go and see whose destiny is being shaped down there."

Chapter 22

Pearl was so angry with herself for failing to save Emmie, so angry with Emmie for not wanting to be saved and so angry with Thomas for absolutely everything which had happened that day, that she didn't talk or listen or try to learn. She just concentrated on getting out of the corrie, to the boulders and bracken at the foot of the Keystone Peak.

Everyone around her had powers she didn't understand. But she did know she had to stop Thomas gathering all three triplets in one place.

She didn't know what would happen if they crowned the Earl, but the Laird's snide comments and Thomas's silence suggested the triplets would be in danger.

And she did know she couldn't go home and leave the triplets to face danger without her.

They reached the wall which marked the boundary of the Laird's land and turned east towards the River Stane. Pearl glanced back at Emmie, who was smiling up at Thomas, asking him another admiring question.

The triplets used to look at Pearl like that. Now Pearl had nothing to offer them. Except an alternative to Thomas's destiny.

Thomas had promised Pearl the chance to show her brother and sisters they had a choice. She didn't have glamour or music or power, but perhaps she could persuade them with common sense. Or perhaps she needed a more dramatic argument.

They reached the hole Thomas had blasted in the wall.

"Now what?" Pearl demanded, speaking to Thomas and her sister for the first time since they left the Keystone Peak.

Thomas answered, "Now we find my grandfather, reunite the triplets, capture the Laird — who I hope is still lying under the wreck of his ballroom — then march up to Landlaw Hold for the crowning ceremony."

Pearl looked up and saw the old castle on the side of the Anvil, broken and crumbling, but still powerful. The keep crouched above them like a sharp grey beast defending its territory. Pearl closed her eyes briefly.

"You don't have to come, Pearl," murmured Thomas. "I don't need you, and I haven't promised you to my grandfather. You can go home if you want."

Pearl turned to Emmie, who nodded. "I'm sure I'll manage on my own." But her hand slipped into Pearl's and she grasped her big sister's fingers.

Pearl looked directly at Thomas. "You promised I could tell the triplets that there's no such thing as destiny. If I come with you, will I have a chance to argue my case? And once they've heard me, if they choose to, can they come home with me? Can they decide for themselves?"

"I gave you my word, Pearl, so yes, you can make your case, and yes, they can choose. I'm confident they'll choose their destiny, but if every single triplet wants to go home with you, I won't stop them, and I won't let my grandfather stop them. However, if even one of them wants to follow their destiny, then all of them must link hands and crown my grandfather.

"You would have to persuade all three of them, Pearl. Can you do that? They don't often do what you tell them, do they?"

Pearl thought of Ruby's tears, Emmie's fascination with the lore and Jasper's admiration for Thomas. But she forced a smile and said, "We'll let them decide."

As they clambered over the rubble of the fallen wall, Emmie asked, "So where do we go to find Ruby and Jasper?"

"My grandfather's hornblast came from the Stane Bridge. We'd better get there before he gets impatient."

So they didn't head for the pink and yellow castle, saggy and squint in the distance. They walked briskly southeast towards the River Stane.

"How can he be sure you'll come?" asked Emmie. "After all, you very nearly didn't catch us."

"He knows I keep my word, and I promised to deliver you all to him in return for the ancient lorefast."

"Deliver them!" snorted Pearl. "You can't deliver them! They're people, not parcels."

"Return them, if you prefer. Return them to their rightful owner, the man who created them."

Emmie stopped and looked at Thomas. "Created us? What do you mean?"

Thomas smiled. "You didn't know about that? Pearl didn't tell you? She seemed interested enough earlier."

Emmie glared at Pearl, then turned to Thomas again. "But what did he create us *for?*"

Thomas laughed. "Have neither of you worked out what our three jewels are for yet? The Horsburghs don't need to search for the keystone any more, because we're forging our own new link to the mountains.

"Our new link is a crown. A crown of gemstones.

"A crown of Ruby, Jasper and Emerald.

"So my grandfather's three precious gems will give him all the power and music of the mountains."

"They aren't your grandfather's gems," insisted Pearl. "They don't belong to anyone!" Her voice rose until she was almost shouting.

Thomas held up his hands at Pearl's passion. "Don't argue with me, Pearl, it's your family you need to persuade."

Pearl looked at the sister by her side. Emmie was very pale, glancing quickly back at the Keystone Peak.

"Oh!" said Pearl suddenly. "But you don't need …"

Emmie grabbed her arm and whispered, "Don't tell him. I think the keystone is more powerful for us as a secret, don't you?"

"I don't need what?" Thomas asked, puzzled.

"Er … you don't need me any more," Pearl stuttered. Then she added wistfully, "No one needs me any more."

Thomas frowned, but Emmie smiled at him and asked, "Do you think my white horse will be waiting at the bridge?"

So Thomas led them over a slight rise, where they could see the bridge, the river, and on the far bank, a small group of people and horses.

Pearl saw the widest figure clamber on the tallest horse and gallop over the bridge. The huge black horse thundered towards them as heavily as a carthorse, but stopped in front of them as precisely as a competitor in the dressage ring. The stallion's rider leapt off and flung his arms round Thomas.

"My boy, my boy! I knew you wouldn't let me down. I knew you would keep your promises."

The Earl of Horsburgh was dressed, like Thomas, for the hunt. But his hairy green tweeds were baggy, unflattering and several decades out of date, whereas Thomas still looked sharp and fashionable even after a day on the hills.

The Earl grinned widely, showing large yellow teeth in his broad red face, and he waggled his bristly ginger eyebrows at Pearl and Emmie. Pearl took a step back. He was jolly, welcoming and absolutely terrifying.

"So, who do we have here?" he asked as he handed Thomas the reins of his horse. "Who *do* we have here?" he repeated, bending down and pinching Emmie's cheeks.

"You must be Emerald. The third gemstone in my crown. What a gorgeous little thing you are." He grabbed Emmie's small white hand with his large brown one and shook it up and down.

He slapped Thomas on the shoulder. "Well done. Well done. You've given me them all. Aren't they lovely!"

He patted Emmie on the head. "Plenty of time to make friends later, dear little Emerald. Right now we have to catch the bad man and take him to the big grey castle. Then there might be time for cream cakes and ginger beer, do you think, Thomas?" He strode off towards the bridge.

Thomas smiled affectionately at his grandfather's wide back, then led the black horse after him. Pearl and Emmie followed, a safe distance behind the large dark hooves.

Thomas called out, "Emerald isn't just lovely, my lord, she's already able to hold and use the power of the land. Don't underestimate her."

"Really? How wonderful!" the Earl yelled over his shoulder. "The more power the better, I always say."

Emmie giggled, then whispered, "What a strange man! He thinks if he's hearty and enthusiastic, he'll make us all join in without asking any questions. I wonder if it worked with Jasper and Ruby?" Pearl shrugged, but she was afraid it might have done.

"And who is this?" The Earl suddenly whirled round and bared his teeth in a snarling grin at Pearl. "Another triplet? Surely not. That would make four, and you've always been better at arithmetic than that, Thomas."

"I am Pearl. I am the oldest Chayne sister." Pearl stood firm under the Earl's heavy stare. "I've come to take my brother and sisters home."

"Have you indeed? Thomas?" The Earl looked to

his grandson for an explanation.

Thomas shrugged. "She doesn't hear the land. The land doesn't hear her."

"Ah," said the Earl, and immediately turned his back on Pearl.

Soon, Thomas and the Earl were talking in low voices ahead, so Pearl leant closer to Emmie and muttered, "You aren't going to take part in this crowning, are you? You do have a plan?"

"I think so."

"You only think so? Because if you can't use your fancy music to get us away from these madmen, I'm just going to throw you all on that great big horse and ride us out of here."

"Don't be daft. His horse won't do what you say. Anyway, if we run, they'll chase us. If we make it home, they'll steal us again. We have to finish this today, or we'll never be safe from them."

"Finish it how?"

"We have to make our own destiny."

They crossed the humpbacked bridge to the gathering of four horses and two children.

Thomas rushed to the only horse Pearl didn't recognise, a muscular dappled grey almost as tall as his grandfather's black. Thomas spoke softly to her, then leapt on her back.

Pearl recognised the three other gleaming, snorting, stamping horses. The warm stable smell of the Horsburghs' mounts mingled with the scent of woodshavings and walnut oil from three cold wooden rocking horses.

The palomino rocking horse stood beside Ruby; the chestnut stallion stood beside Jasper. The Earl walked Emmie over to the white mare and lined the triplets up in front of their horses. "You are all so perfect. So exactly as I wanted you. My precious stones."

They did look like a matched set of gemstones, unblemished and exactly alike. But Pearl could see their eyes: Ruby looking down at the ground; Jasper gazing up at Thomas; and Emmie looking past everyone else at the mountains.

When the Earl turned to get on his horse, Ruby and Jasper greeted Emmie with hugs, but looked nervously at Pearl.

Pearl stepped close to Ruby, who was stroking the palomino's nose. "I thought you hated that nasty beast."

Ruby slid behind the mare's shoulder. "She let me groom her."

Pearl shook her head. "And who did I say you should open the door for?" Ruby bit her lip and the tip of her nose turned red.

"Did I say you should open it for wolves? Or strange men? *Or sneaky treacherous little brothers?*"

She turned on Jasper. "And you! Why did you help the Earl? Why did you help him steal your sister?"

Jasper stood tall and confident. "Because they will teach me to use my power. Because the normal rules don't apply to people like us."

"Honour? Loyalty? Honesty? They don't apply?"

Jasper flinched. "You don't understand, Pearl. You're trying to save us from something we want! Just leave us alone. We're in good hands."

Pearl looked at the Horsburghs, high on their horses, reins held negligently in their fingers.

The Earl laughed. "The land doesn't listen to her, Thomas, and neither does anyone else! Ha! Ha ha!"

Thomas laughed with his grandfather, but kept his face turned away from Pearl.

"Ready, troops?" bellowed the Earl. "Time to capture the Laird."

Chapter 23

The triplets climbed on their horses, and all five riders set off for Swanhaugh Towers. Pearl was left standing alone on the riverbank. Had they forgotten her? For a moment she hoped they had, then Emmie reined in her horse on the bridge and asked if Pearl wanted to ride with her.

Pearl pulled herself up onto the shining white rocking horse and sat perched on the back of the red leather saddle. Her legs gripped the mare's hard flanks. The horse cantered after the others.

The Earl led the way, but Thomas held his horse back to ride behind the triplets. If it was a precaution to stop the triplets escaping, it was unnecessary: Emmie's white horse followed the Earl's black like a foal follows its dam.

The rocking horse cantered with the same rhythm as a real horse. But the creaking as the mare stretched, and the echoing boom as each hoof hit the ground, reminded Pearl she was sitting on a hollow wooden horse.

Though Pearl had never approved of these unnatural creations, she enjoyed the speed, after a day of slogging up and down hills on her own tired feet.

Earlier in the afternoon, Pearl had thought

the Laird's castle looked uncared for; as she hurtled towards it this time, it looked broken. The towers were now squint, the front door was blown outwards and the walls bulged.

The Earl pulled his horse to a halt just a few steps from the columns struggling to hold up the front of the castle. The three rocking horses slammed to a stop in a perfect line behind him.

"Where is he, my boy?" roared the Earl.

"I pinned him down under the minstrels' gallery," answered Thomas. "And I shattered his lorefast, so he has nothing but his skinny old arms to help him escape. He'll still be there."

"Are you sure he isn't dead?"

"I hope not. I didn't mean to kill him. You know how Mother feels ... felt ... about using death or bloodlore. I just walled him in so we could dig him out later. But it will need both of us, my lord, one to get him out and the other to control him. So we'll have to take the children in with us, or they might ..." Thomas frowned at Pearl, "... they might wander off."

Everyone slid from their horses. Pearl said, "You can't take children in there. It could collapse in the slightest breeze."

Thomas laughed. "It might not last a Perthshire winter, but I think we can tiptoe in on a summer afternoon. If you're scared, Pearl, stay out here. But the triplets are coming with me. Come and see what happens to our enemies, children. Bring the rocking horses. We might need their strength."

He marched towards the southern wing of Swanhaugh Towers, followed by his grandfather, the triplets and the rocking horses. Pearl walked behind them. As she turned the corner, she saw her family enter the castle through an uneven archway blasted out of the ballroom wall, exactly where she and Emmie had stood watching the rat's blood feed the earth.

Pearl stepped cautiously over the rubble and into the ballroom. The wooden floor was scarred by jagged lumps of stone fallen from the walls and ceilings. Coloured glass and lead from the windows lay in drifts at each corner.

The minstrels' gallery above her head had come away from the wall at one end and was still attached at the other, so it hung down like an impossible staircase with no steps.

The gallery on the other side, where Pearl and Thomas had first watched Emmie fly, had collapsed onto the ground in one piece. It formed a solid fence, blocking off the far side of the room.

"He's under there." Thomas pointed to the fallen wooden platform. "If we harness the rocking horses, they can haul it away. Do you have any rope in those pockets of yours, Pearl? No? Then I'll use this." He walked to a smashed window and started ripping down the golden ropes which looped the curtains to the wall.

"Isn't he wonderful?" the Earl called to the whole room. "Just wonderful."

Emmie was describing the chase in the air to Ruby and Jasper, swooping her hands high, keeping her voice low. They gazed at her, looking up even though they were all the same height.

Pearl had no one to talk to, no one to admire. She stared at the floor, poking the toes of her scuffed boots into the debris: slices of dark varnished wood from the carved ceiling; crystals from the chandeliers, grey with years of grime; fistfuls of crumbling plaster; and, still shiny and clean because they lay on top of the dust, a couple of long white feathers.

Pearl tilted her head up. Through ragged holes in the ceiling she could see painted walls in the room above.

She turned towards her brother and sisters. "Get out!" she mouthed soundlessly, gesturing with her hands, trying not to draw the attention of Thomas, the Earl or the rocking horses.

"Get out now!" But the triplets were too busy discussing the Laird and the mountains to notice her.

Pearl's eyes flicked between the ceiling and the people scattered round the ballroom. The triplets were chatting in the middle of the dancefloor. The Earl was throwing a golden rope round the stallion's chest, and Thomas was crouching down, tying the other end to struts of the overturned gallery.

Pearl saw a white blur move across the hole just above her. She looked back down to the dancefloor. Thomas's head was bent, his long pale neck exposed to the air above.

Pearl couldn't bear it.

"Swans!" she yelled. "There are swans up there!"

The horses reared, the children leapt apart, and Thomas whirled up and round.

Then the noise began.

First a hoarse scream from under the collapsed gallery.

Then a thrumming, vibrating, churring noise from above, like thousands of fingers stroking thousands of drums.

The holes in the ceiling filled with white movement.

Pearl flinched, expecting hundreds of swans to swoop down in violent v-shapes. But nothing came down except a few feathers. The white shapes stayed in one place, beating their wings.

She stared up, not understanding what the birds were doing.

But Thomas understood, and said calmly, "Pearl, get the children into the fireplace."

The fireplace? She was confused, wondering if she'd mentioned Hansel and Gretel out loud today. She didn't want to push anyone into an oven or a fireplace.

The thrumming was getting louder.

"*Now,* Pearl!" he yelled.

Pearl used her outstretched arms to guide the triplets ahead of her into the huge fireplace.

Soot coated the wide chimney above them, charred wood from small fires darkened the stone underneath. Their shifting feet crunched on burnt bones.

She judged the distance from the fireplace to the hole in the wall. Could she get the triplets out while Thomas and the Earl were busy?

Thomas was working frantically to secure a third rope to the gallery, and his grandfather was trying to keep the palomino calm so she could take the strain and pull the gallery forward.

Before Pearl could choose the best escape route across the floor, her view of the exit was blocked. Now it wasn't just feathers floating into the ballroom. Dust and specks of plaster were spiralling down.

"Why aren't Thomas and the Earl fighting back?" whined Jasper. "Surely they're more powerful than those birds?"

Pearl shook her head. She'd finally worked it out. "The swans are beating their wings to make the rafters and plaster shake, to bring the whole ballroom ceiling down on our heads. If the Horsburghs fight back like Thomas fought the Laird, their power will pull the whole castle down."

Emmie added, "So they're just trying to shift the gallery as fast as they can."

Ruby snivelled. "That thumping noise is giving me a headache."

"Then let's get out of here. Everyone grab hands." Pearl seized Jasper's hand and tried to drag him out of the fireplace. Jasper yanked his hand away and cowered into a corner of the chimney.

The three horses pulled together and the gallery groaned and shifted.

The ceiling fell in.

And Pearl's world turned grey.

Black soot poured onto the children in the fireplace. White dust exploded to fill the whole ballroom. Great weights crashed through the clouds to smash on the floor. Finally the clumsy shapes of swans swooped down and out of the broken wall.

Everything was silent. The dust drifted down slowly and the air cleared.

Pearl wiped her eyes on her cuffs. The floor of the ballroom looked like a model landscape: long mountain ranges of rafters and glacial valleys of snowy dust. But no movement.

Then she heard a cough, and looked over to where the Horsburghs had been working. The gallery was a few steps further from the wall. Several dusty hills started to move in front of it.

Thomas stood up, wiped his face on a handkerchief, and pointed his staff towards a heap by the wall. "Up!" he commanded, and the Laird uncurled his skinny length from the floor.

Then the Earl stamped himself free of dust and pointed his hunting horn at the Laird. "Out!" he ordered. "And keep those swans at a distance."

The Laird snarled, but picked his way across the floor towards the hole in the wall.

Pearl started to lead the triplets out too: Ruby sneezing, Jasper grinning, Emmie staring up at the few remaining rafters.

The white mare and the chestnut stallion sprang from the rubble and flicked their dusty tails. They trotted out to the grass, where they both lay down and rolled their flanks clean.

Pearl looked round. Where was the third horse?

She saw a feeble movement by the gallery and ran over.

The palomino was trapped under a lump of carved stone, the huge weight lying across her belly and back legs.

This was the horse Pearl had fooled with a mirror; the horse whose golden bridle ring had led her to Thomas and started this day's journey; the horse who had tried to trample her in the deer forest. Pearl knew she was a vain, violent beast. But now the mare lay gasping at her feet, crushed between the hard wood floor and the heavy stone block.

Pearl couldn't move the stone. She wasn't strong enough to lift it, and she didn't want to hurt the horse by rocking it off.

Pearl blew lightly to shift the fine grit from the horse's face, then blew harder to reveal the damage on her flank.

The horse's wooden body was splintered. Sharp points of broken wood jutted up through the saddlecloth.

Thomas crouched down beside Pearl, moving his fingers expertly over the mare's side and belly. After a look under her saddle, he sat back on his heels and just put his hand gently on her neck.

Ruby ran up to them, and stroked the horse's nose. The mare's rattling breathing slowed. The rasp of her broken ribs scraping together quietened.

The horse lay still. Suddenly completely still.

Pearl watched as the varnish on the horse's sides faded and flaked. Her eyes, open and staring, lost their wet shine, and her limbs became stiff.

Ruby wailed. Pearl put her arms round her little sister and hugged her.

The low evening sunlight sliding through the shattered windows shone on a discarded toy:

carved, painted and varnished, then used, broken and thrown away.

Pearl stretched out her hand to close the horse's eyelids. They didn't move. They were made of solid wood.

Chapter 24

The three children knelt by the rigid wooden horse.

Thomas took the gold ring from his waistcoat and placed it by the rocking horse's neck. It turned once, then lay down. He said quietly, "Let's get out of here; it's not safe."

Pearl hissed at him, "It was never safe."

He just repeated, his voice flat. "Let's get out of here."

As they left the ballroom, the Earl put his hand on Thomas's shoulder. "Sorry, my boy."

"Why are you sorry?" Pearl said bitterly. "You gave false life to these creatures, you forced them into danger, then took that life away. Is that what you've done with the triplets? Created lives for your own selfish ends, planning to take them away?"

The Earl glanced at her, then turned to Thomas. "Why is she still here? She annoys me. Come and secure Swanhaugh for me."

Thomas took one last look at the ballroom floor and walked out of the castle past his grandfather and the Laird, who was still controlled by the constant threat of the Earl's lorefast.

Thomas picked a handful of pliable green reeds

from the edge of the nearest canal, sat down and began to pleat them into a rope.

Pearl stood protectively beside the triplets, as Ruby wept and Emmie comforted her. But Jasper sauntered over to Thomas. "Can I help?"

Thomas looked up sharply, and Pearl thought he was going to snap at Jasper for disturbing him. But he nodded. "Yes, you can fetch me more reeds."

By the time Jasper brought more, Thomas had finished the length of rope. He smiled at Jasper, and added one of his reeds anyway.

Thomas wound the rope round his lorefast, like a vine round a post or a snake round a branch. Then, holding his staff at the top, he pulled the rope steadily so it slithered all the way down the length of the staff.

Then he approached the Laird, threw the green rope around the old man's arms and chest, tied it swiftly in a simple knot and stood back. "Now my power holds you prisoner," he said with satisfaction.

The Laird tried to move his arms, but couldn't.

"Follow me," ordered Thomas, and walked off. The Laird moved after him, lurching from side to side as he tried to resist the boy's command.

Pearl was suddenly glad Thomas had chosen to persuade the triplets, rather than force them, to follow him.

Thomas led the Laird in a circle back towards the Earl. "Stop," ordered Thomas, and the Laird stopped.

The Earl laughed. "Good work! Good work indeed."

Thomas gave a tight smile, then turned to the triplets. "Now it's time to go to the castle."

"They're not going to the castle," Pearl said firmly.

Thomas raised his eyebrows.

"You gave me your word that I would get a chance to persuade the triplets your nasty little plan isn't their destiny. And you promised that if I persuaded them all, we could go home. Now I want my chance."

"You promised her *what?*" boomed the Earl. "You promised a child who cannot even hear the land the chance to argue against my gemstones' destiny and my rights?

"Thomas Horsburgh," his voice fell to a threatening purr, "Thomas Horsburgh, you disappoint me."

"I needed her help and it was an honest bargain." Thomas's voice was calm. "Anyway, it seems right to give the children a sporting chance, doesn't it? Given what's at stake."

"What do you think is at stake, boy? My right to the crown, or your right to the Landlaw lorefast? What is at stake? What are you gambling with?"

"Actually," Thomas said icily, "I meant what is at stake for *them.*"

The Earl glared at Thomas.

"Anyway," the tall boy shrugged, "if it really is their destiny, nothing she says can change it, can it?"

The Earl nodded once, so Thomas smiled at the triplets and invited them to sit with him on the bank of the canal. Then he looked expectantly at Pearl. "The floor is yours."

But Pearl had seen her father in the law courts

and knew how to get a slim advantage in debate. "No. You're proposing a destiny for them; I'm opposing it. You speak first."

Thomas laughed. "A lawyer as well as a hunter!"

He leapt up, strode a few steps away and turned to face the triplets. Pearl sat down beside Emmie. The Earl stood beside the captive Laird. As Thomas took a deep breath, his grandfather snorted, "Play-acting!"

But Thomas looked very serious as he began to speak. "Emerald. Ruby. Jasper. I want to show you three things. I want to show that this is your destiny, because you were created to crown the Earl. I want to show that if you turn your back on your destiny, you risk giving the mountains to a man who will misuse their power. Finally I want to show how glorious that destiny can be. Then the choice will be yours." He held his hands out to the triplets.

Pearl groaned softly. She'd made a dreadful mistake. She'd created the perfect platform for a boy who'd already half-enchanted each child with his charm and fancy tricks. She'd agreed to a contest stacked against her from the start: she had to persuade all three children to win; Thomas only had to persuade one. She looked at their eager faces gazing at him and groaned again.

"I call my first witness," Thomas said, the lilt in his voice betraying how much fun he was having. "Kenneth Horsburgh, Earl of this county, will you step forward?"

"Nonsense," harrumphed the Earl, but he looked pleased to be asked and walked forward to face Thomas.

"My lord, have you seen these children before?"

Pearl coughed to hide a nervous laugh. Would the Earl take a tiny notebook out of a pocket and consult it, like a police constable in the Sheriff Court?

"No," answered the Earl.

"But do you know of them?"

"Oh yes. I knew of them before they were born."

"Can you explain?"

"Well," the Earl stood with his thumbs in his braces and leant back into the air, as if he was telling a tale by his own fireplace, "well, my daughter-in-law, your mother, Thomas, was a bit of a folklorist in her spare time. Loved to listen to the land, but also loved to listen to how the local folk tried to call on our power in their ham-fisted, half-hearted, ignorant, superstitious way. Jane knew I found them amusing, but I think she was fond of them.

"Anyway, during the Great War she brought me information she thought I might find interesting. The wife of one of my neighbours had just lost a son in the war, and as the mother of one remaining baby daughter, she was desperate for more children. She didn't want the little girl to grow up alone, said my daughter-in-law. She was trying everything: getting up at dawn and tying ribbons to rowan trees; throwing coins to the spirit of the river; even, in a garbled sort of way, offering the souls of her unborn children to the powers around her, if only she could have more children. Of course, she didn't get any of the words right, she threw gold when she should have thrown silver, she faced the wrong way, and stood in the wrong place, and sneezed at just the wrong time, so we could have ignored her requests completely. But Jane knew I was laying the groundwork for my conquest of the Laird and my victory in the mountains, and thought this woman might be useful.

"We don't have to grant the requests of those who can't hear the land, but when it suits our own ends, we do grant wishes. Though I don't look much like a fairy godmother, do I?"

The Earl laughed heartily at his own joke. Pearl realised her teeth were clamped together; she looked at the triplets, white-faced, gripping each other's hands. They were all beginning to understand why Mother avoided the neighbours to the south.

The Earl slapped himself on the chest to stop his chuckles, and continued his story.

"So on midsummer morning, the woman came to the riverbank, cut a lock of her own hair, and said, 'I'd give anything if I could bear more children.' Jane appeared cloaked in morning mist and asked if she really meant *anything*. When the woman sank to her knees and begged for more children, Jane said she could have three if she would let them have a destiny far greater than her other children, and if she would free them to that destiny when it was time. She agreed. So Jane gave the foolish woman a bag of herbs to help her get pregnant one more time. As she walked away from the water, I sent powers spinning after her to wait in her belly for her children: the deepest landlore I could summon, the strongest potential links to the mountains I could forge, and the power to crown the next lord in the castle of Landlaw Hold.

"And so," he towered over the sitting children with a hungry grin, "and so, I made you. You are mine. Because your mother gave you to me."

He stepped back to leave the floor to Thomas, but Emmie asked quickly, "Did you send the power of flight spinning into her belly?"

He frowned at her and shook his head.

"So who did?"

The Laird cleared his throat, and they all turned to look at him. He smirked.

"Perhaps you didn't create us all by yourself, and have no claim over us," Emmie said to the Earl with a charming smile.

"Whatever unnatural powers you had grafted onto you, you were my idea. If I hadn't needed you, your mother would never have had you. Without me, you would not exist!" He walked off triumphantly.

Pearl patted Emmie on the shoulder, but they didn't look at each other. They were staring at Thomas, who thanked his grandfather, then announced, "I call my second witness, the Laird of Swanhaugh."

The Laird walked nonchalantly towards the children, as if he'd chosen to step forward.

Thomas spoke softly. "There are three possibilities for the mountains: first, no one takes responsibility for them and they fade away into silence; second, you crown my grandfather so he can use his power and their music to care for them;

or finally, this Laird uses you to crown himself, then he takes control. But what would the Laird do with that power?

"Swanhaugh." He coughed the name up as if it tasted foul. "Swanhaugh, tell us about bloodlore."

The Laird spoke very quietly, but no one, not even the horses, moved as he spoke, so they heard every word.

"As you know, Tommy boy, bloodlore adds the power of the living creature to the power of the land. You cut open a vein and let the blood sink in. And as the creature dies, the land lives. The hot wet red blood calls back memories of molten rock more vividly than your waltzes and polkas. Land watered with blood resists the nasty fingers of weathering. Land fed with blood seeks more blood."

"Do you use bloodlore?" asked Thomas.

"Yes I do," leered the Laird.

"Does anyone else in this county?"

"No. Your weak-willed branch of the family called it barbaric and declared it taboo. So you perch on top of the land, singing little ditties to it, and you never reach to the heights nor dive to the depths of the power our ancestors had. You never feel the earth in your veins, nor breathe the sky into your lungs. You're too bothered about rules and responsibility to *enjoy* landlore."

Thomas shook his head. "But you're so addicted to bloodletting and flying that you forget simple responsibilities like sheep shearing and grass cutting. You're not fit to care for the land if you just care about your own pleasures."

The Laird laughed. "Bloodlore isn't just about pleasure, Thomas. It's about power too. Power and death. Don't forget that."

Pearl noticed dozens of swans circling far behind the Laird. But they came no nearer than the edge of the parklands.

Thomas spoke slowly. "I haven't forgotten that. Did you use bloodlore three summers ago?"

"You remember that, little Tommy?" The Laird's voice flowed like warm grease. "I killed a whole herd of deer that summer, and drenched the land at the north side of the Keystone Peak. The flood of blood sliced off a whole cliff. I heard the mountain scream and I heard you scream too, boy, when you found your mother. I got the Horsburgh hind that day, but not the calf. I was aiming for you then, and I know my swans nearly got you earlier today. Keep looking around you, above and below. I'll get you eventually. If I don't, one of my kin in the bloodlore will."

Thomas was very pale by the end of the Laird's answer, but his voice was still steady. "Did you use bloodlore this morning?"

"I hardly needed to. Your gutless horses fled at the first sight of my swans. Those children's toys were split from each other with no more than a few drops of mousy blood in the woods. And the white mare's hooves were persuaded onto the path towards my lands with nothing but a couple of bones bent into horseshoes and a bit of smoke from the top of the Anvil. Then I covered her tracks and my own with a breath of rain.

"But I admit, I did bleed a few hares dry round

the rocks above my Towers, just in case anyone came sneaking and spying. I forced the rocks to twist and turn to my tune, and you very nearly joined in the dance, little girl, didn't you?" He leant towards Pearl, his tongue poking at the gaps in his rotting teeth. "Perhaps I'll get you next time."

"You won't get her," Thomas said sharply. "You won't get anyone ever again. Not if these children accept their destiny."

He faced the triplets and opened his arms. "If you choose not to crown my grandfather, do you think the Laird will give you a choice about whether you crown him? Do you want to let him feed the land with death rather than life? Do you want to let him use his power to force the land to do his bidding? Do you want to let a man like him, and a lore like that, loose on the mountains?"

"It's not that simple," broke in the Laird. "You call bloodlore taboo, but there are ways of hurting living things without spilling blood." He whirled round to face the triplets. "Ask him how their ritual ..."

But Thomas flicked his staff at the green rope round Swanhaugh's chest and it tightened so fast the Laird couldn't finish the sentence.

"Thank you for your testimony. Return to your place." The Laird walked stiffly back to the Earl.

"My third witness is ... the land."

Thomas crouched down in front of his audience. "I want you to feel the rhythm of the rocks, the pulse of the earth, and I want you to know you'll lose that music forever if you don't follow me up to the castle tonight."

Pearl saw the triplets' eyes fixed eagerly on Thomas as he stood up. "Grandfather, I'm sure you agree I will demonstrate our skills and power far more effectively with the Landlaw lorefast." He walked towards his grandfather. "After all, I have delivered everything I promised you."

He held out his hand.

The Earl hesitated.

Thomas said in a slow melodic voice, "With the lorefast, I can give them to you as willing participants. You know what that's worth."

"Clever," whispered Emmie to Pearl. "He is very clever, isn't he?"

"I gave him the perfect excuse to ask," muttered Pearl. "Sorry."

The Earl nodded his decision. "Of course, of course, dear boy. You've exceeded my expectations, and I'm sure you're worthy of it."

The Earl took from his jacket pocket, not a little notebook, but a wooden box the size of his fist. He opened it and offered it to Thomas, whose long fingers prised out a crescent-shaped black shell. After a quiet moment holding the shell on his palm, Thomas lifted it up high so the dull black flickered with stripes as wrinkles on its surface caught the light.

Pearl recognised it as a freshwater mussel from the pebbly beds of one of the local rivers, held closed with a thin piece of faded twine. When Thomas shook it gently, there was a soft rolling sound.

"There's a pearl in there," murmured Emmie.

Thomas strode over to the children and knelt down beside Pearl. With a smile like he had eaten all the jam in the pantry and found someone else to blame, he whispered so only Pearl could hear.

"Thank you, quiet girl, quiet Pearl. You and your petty little debate about destiny have given me what I always wanted. And you said your name meant nothing!"

Chapter 25

Thomas lashed the delicate shell to his staff with one of Jasper's reeds. He moved a few paces away and turned on the spot, looking first at the grass under his feet, then at the water snaking around them, and finally looking up to the mountains.

He laughed, then pointed his finger straight at the Laird. The Laird flinched; the Earl moved slightly away.

"Swanhaugh, you spend so much time flapping in air and splashing in blood that you've neglected your own garden. Let's tidy it up for you."

Thomas began to move his wooden staff. Pearl recognised the twisting motion of his wrist, but this time it was slower, gentler, and the pearl inside the shell was rattling and rolling softly, playing a high watery note. Thomas drew growing circles with the staff, and the shell's music got louder.

He spoke clearly above it. "You've seen us use the power of the land in anger and fear, now let me show you how to use it with love and respect."

He flicked the lorefast at the canal beside them. As the familiar boom reached her, Pearl jerked, ready to wrap her arms round her head. But the wave of sound wasn't violent this time, it was warm and resonating, and it was joined by the light music of the shell. As they vibrated in unison, Thomas added his voice, flowing round the percussion of the staff.

As he sang, the weed-choked water began to flow in circles, in time with the twisting of the staff. As it moved, the clumps of leaves and algae sank to the bottom and vanished. The dark water cleared, until it was reflecting the pure blue of the late evening sky.

Thomas held out his free hand. "Jasper, will you help me?"

Jasper leapt to his feet, ran to grab Thomas's hand, and joined his higher voice to the song. Thomas lifted his staff and drew in the air the shape of all the waterways in the meadow. Soon the sweet smell of clean water spread over the whole haugh.

"Ruby, would you like to ..." Before he finished, Ruby jumped up and grabbed Jasper's hand. Thomas changed the notes of his song and twisted his staff at the nearest canal again.

Stunted grey fish, so pale they were almost see-through, leapt out of the water. They flew in an arc through the air, growing longer and plumper, their scales shining with silvery rainbows. Then they dived back into the sparkling water, splashing Pearl, who was still sitting on the bank.

But there was no one beside Pearl to share her soaking. Emmie had already joined her brother and sister.

As Thomas, Ruby and Jasper sang colours and health into all the fish in the canals, Emmie called over the music, "I don't like that," pointing to the Laird's castle.

"I don't either," laughed Thomas. "What shall we do with it?"

"Hide it," said Emmie.

So Thomas thrust his staff into the grass and sang a different song, joined by all three Chayne triplets. He used both hands to draw branches growing from the lorefast, and a line of dark green appeared in front of Swanhaugh Towers. A hedge of pine trees grew up round the castle, sprouting as fast as the children could sing, hiding all but the tallest towers from view.

Thomas pulled the staff out, and dug his heel into the tangled grass. "Shall we make the grass dance?" he asked. "Yes!" cried the triplets.

Now the beat of the staff and the notes from the shell played faster, more cheerfully, like a military march. Pearl thought it just needed bagpipes to sound like the local regiment recruiting farm boys at the Highland Games. Then the Earl stood behind Thomas and played skirling notes on the bull's horn. Pearl snorted in amusement.

When they started to sing this new tune, the triplets didn't wait for Thomas. They all knew the song, or they made it up together.

As Pearl crouched by the side of the newly fresh canal, she saw the grass start to move, ripples flickering across it like tiny waves on a loch. At first she thought the grass was blowing in a sudden breeze, then she realised the grass was rippling because the ground underneath was crawling and jumping.

Pearl remembered the terror of the shifting rocks on the Keystone Peak, and how Emmie had saved her there. Pearl watched Emmie now, her mouth a perfect circle, working with Thomas to move the earth. Who would save her this time?

Thomas had one hand flat, holding a piece of ground behind him steady for the Laird and the four horses, who were shifting their hooves nervously.

Thomas and the Earl were lifted and swung carefully by the earth as if it held them in its hands. They smiled at the triplets, who had stepped onto the most vigorously moving grass.

The children kept losing their place in the song, shrieking with laughter as they bounced and bumped into each other. Ruby fell over and pulled Jasper down with her. Emmie kept her footing with her arms out like wings.

The circle of moving grass widened towards Pearl. As she stood up, she caught Thomas staring at her. He pointed to the still island behind him, but she didn't want his help. She placed her feet wide apart, held her head up, and rode the pulsing waves of earth. She was flung upwards, then the earth vanished and she dropped down, but she didn't lose her balance.

The waves sweeping through the grass were like a brush through matted hair, smoothing and tidying the green blades. Moss, nettles and dandelions vanished, replaced by buttercups and daisies, already closing for the night.

Thomas murmured, "Shshsh." The triplets stopped shrieking and singing, the Earl blew a last note on his horn, the grass shivered and lay still.

Pearl stood steady on her feet and crossed her arms.

Thomas flung his arms wide and cried, "See what we have done!"

Pearl looked reluctantly round at a beautiful pleasure garden: fresh water, smooth lawns, a mature wood with a couple of towers peeping above the trees.

"Did you enjoy that?" he asked the triplets.

They were breathless, but nodding.

"If you want to feel that glorious power again, come with me and crown the Earl."

Before they could answer, Thomas held up a hand. "It's only fair to let your sister have her say first." He sat down, folding his long legs, and putting his staff and its shell carefully beside him.

"Your turn, Pearl."

Chapter 26

The triplets tumbled happily into a heap beside Thomas. The Laird and the Earl stood watching Pearl critically. The horses wandered off, the black and the grey already nibbling at the fresh new grass.

Pearl felt grubby, sweaty and exhausted, in no state to save her brother and sisters with clever words. However, the argument she wanted to present had been forming in her mind all day as she travelled through the mountains.

She faced Emmie, Ruby and Jasper. "I'm going to persuade you there's no such thing as destiny. I don't have any fairy tales or magic tricks or family singalongs.

"But I do have a witness."

That caught the triplets' attention. They looked round, confused.

"I call as a witness our brother, Peter Chayne."

She swept her hand behind her, as if to usher someone forward. When no one appeared, she looked puzzled and searched over her shoulder.

"Oh, of course. Peter can't be here, can he? Peter can't give evidence to you about destiny and the people who tell you what your destiny is, because Peter is DEAD."

There was a moment's silence. The triplets had stopped tickling and giggling; they looked up at Pearl's tense face.

"Peter is dead because when he was only sixteen years old, he was told it was his destiny to fight for his country. Told by politicians in the newspapers, by ministers in the church, by women in the street who gave white feathers to schoolboys. He was told it was his destiny to kill people he didn't know, on the orders of other people he didn't know.

"Because he believed it was his destiny, and because he believed destiny was glorious, Peter lied about his age, joined a Glasgow regiment where no one would recognise him and was killed in his first week in France, probably shot by someone who thought he was fulfilling his own destiny.

"Peter died because he was told it was his destiny to go to war. But it didn't have to be his destiny. If he had waited until he was eighteen, until he was old enough to join up without lying, the Great War would have been over. Then he could have told you himself that you make your own destiny.

"The future is not written anywhere, and even if it was, why would we trust *them* to write it?" She pointed at Thomas, the Earl and the Laird. "We don't know these people, but we know what they do. They destroy buildings, they rip up mountainsides, they mutilate animals, and they try to kill each other and their neighbours' children.

"We can't know what they want with you in that castle tonight, because even if I asked all three of them straight questions, we couldn't trust their answers. We don't know whether it's a midnight feast or a violent sacrifice. All we do know is they've planned your part in it without asking you.

"When someone tells you they know your destiny, it means they want you to do something for them, and they don't think you'll like it. There is no such thing as destiny, there is only the result of the choices you make.

"So your choice is: follow these people who've caused so much destruction and fear in just one day; or refuse to have anything to do with any of them, Horsburghs or Swanns, and come home with me to your own lives."

Pearl walked slowly along the line of triplets.

"Emmie, Jasper, Ruby. I don't have Thomas's spectacular power, but I do love you. They want you to be their tools. I just want you to be my brother and sisters. Please come home with me for supper."

Her voice cracked, and she stopped. She had no more words.

Thomas stood up. "Finished?" She nodded.

He started to say, "So my precious ..." but Pearl interrupted.

"No more speeches. They know what they have to decide."

Three faces, pink-cheeked and framed with curls, glanced at each other then looked back up at the two older children.

Ruby sniffed. "I want to go home. You're lots of fun, Thomas, but Pearl's right. I don't think I trust you." She hid her face in a hanky.

"Emmie?" asked Pearl tentatively. If Emmie

voted with Ruby, perhaps Jasper would simply go along with his sisters.

"Let Jasper decide next," said Emmie, leaning back on her hands.

Jasper looked at Pearl, then at Thomas, then at the huge chestnut rocking horse. The horse whickered at him.

Jasper spoke clearly. "You might be right, Pearl. Perhaps there is no such thing as destiny." Pearl began to smile.

Her brother raised his voice. "So, if we do have free choice, I choose to be with the Horsburghs and learn to wield the power I deserve."

Thomas breathed a sigh of relief. "One! I only needed one, and they all have to come."

Pearl felt like her skin was crawling over suddenly freezing bones. She gasped, "Emmie! What do you vote?"

"It doesn't matter," said Emmie. "If Jasper goes, we all go. We have to stay together."

"But what would you have voted?" asked Pearl desperately.

Emmie looked calmly at her. "It's probably better if no one knows."

Ruby sobbed, "Pearl, will you stay with us?"

Pearl really didn't want to go up to that dark, jagged stronghold and witness the Horsburghs' ceremony. She glanced at Thomas, who shook his head very slightly. But she said firmly, "If you need me, Ruby, I'll be there."

The Earl instructed the horses to follow the river round the mountains and to go to Horsburgh Hall. Thomas ordered the Laird to start walking.

And in the fading light, Pearl climbed back into the mountains.

As Pearl trailed up the slope, Thomas caught up with her. She slowed down to let him get ahead, but he slowed down too and walked beside her.

He nodded at Jasper, striding out at the front, humming a tune and offering to carry the Earl's jacket. "He has betrayed you at least three times today."

He jerked his head back at Ruby, blowing her nose in a soggy hanky, and he lifted his lip in disgust. "Why don't you just walk away? Why are you doing this for them?"

"Because I'm their big sister." She looked coldly at him. "Why are you doing this *to* them?"

"Because it's my destiny just as much as it is theirs."

"Do you really believe that, Thomas?"

"Yes. Your only witness today was a ghost. I produced real people and real power. I won the argument because destiny is real and you can't fight it."

"We don't know how Emmie would have voted. Perhaps I won."

"You didn't win! You'll never win against me! Emmie didn't tell you how she would have voted because she didn't want to hurt your feelings. I won. They're moving towards their destiny, and if you don't want to watch, you should just go home."

"Thomas, I'm not sure I've understood anything you've said today. But if you really believe the music you sing stops the land decaying, then you don't believe even erosion is inevitable. Nothing is written in stone, not even the future of your rocks. If the earth's destiny isn't fixed, how can the triplets' destiny be fixed? How can yours be, Thomas?"

Pearl took a few faster steps, leaving Thomas frowning behind her. As she strode on, Pearl heard a deep drumming, and looked down at the shining gardens. A flock of swans, elegant at this distance, were flying back to the Laird's lands, beating the air with their wings. They settled down on the dark clean water, fluffing up their pure white feathers.

Chapter 27

The summer sun, which had been with Pearl all day, sank behind the Keystone Peak as they reached Landlaw Hold.

In the sudden dark, Pearl reached out for her sisters' hands. She whispered, "We need a plan."

Emmie answered, "No, we don't. How can we have a plan when we don't know what they're doing?"

"Then we need to tell them that they don't need a crown, because the whole peak is the keystone they're looking for."

"No," said Emmie firmly. "We mustn't tell them that. The Earl won't let us leave here until we've crowned him, whatever we say to him. And we mustn't give them the keystone's power as well as the power of this crown. Let's just wait and see what happens."

"How can you be so naïve?" Pearl snapped. "Just because you can sing their music doesn't mean you can match their power."

"Don't worry, Pearl. All you need to do is stand about with your hands in your pockets."

"Is that all the thanks I get for spending this whole day chasing rocking horses, fighting swans and dodging earthquakes?" Pearl's voice started to rise.

"Shhhh. If the Earl notices you again, he might leave you outside, because he doesn't want a Pearl who can't sing in his crown!" Emmie laughed, an echo of the contempt Pearl had endured from Thomas all day.

Pearl dropped Emmie's hand. She and Ruby followed Jasper and the Earl onto the final approach into the castle.

The girls couldn't have crossed to the castle three abreast anyway. The path was so narrow that two slim children had to put their arms round each others' waists to cross together. Armed men would have had to rush along the path one by one, exposed to the arrowslits in the two front towers for its full forty paces. Pearl imagined attacking the Horsburghs' ancestors here, and shivered.

The ground at their feet, the castle ahead, the sky above, and the drop to the haugh below, were all different shades of grey. They headed towards the only patch of true black: the arched entrance of Landlaw Hold.

Jasper and the Earl entered first, then Ruby and Pearl together, then Emmie on her own, and finally the Laird, shoved through the arch by Thomas.

The courtyard was open to the sky, so they could see each other, but there wasn't enough light for Pearl to see any hiding places or escape routes.

Thomas knelt down by the entrance, picked up a small box, and after a couple of short scrapes, produced a sharp orange spark.

"Jasper, there are dried reed torches behind that pillar. Could you hold them up so I can light them?"

Thomas summoned everyone to take a torch. Pearl kept out of the way, remembering Emmie's warning that the Earl might leave her outside if she made herself noticeable. Soon only Pearl and the Laird had no light of their own.

As the torches warmed and brightened, Pearl could see that the inside of the castle's keep was crumbling too: heaps of rubble in corners, staircases ending halfway up flights, and rooms with missing walls, like empty boxes on their sides. She couldn't see any way out apart from the arched entrance, which led to that dangerously exposed path; nor any places to hide that weren't also traps.

The Earl led the way into the main castle building. Their footsteps sounded hollow as they trailed along a winding corridor towards the turrets at the back.

The Earl ushered them into a huge room, even bigger than the Laird's ballroom, then Thomas twisted a rusty key in the door and put it in his pocket.

Pearl realised this room had been used for much older entertainments than stately ballroom dances. This was a feasting hall, with a raised platform at the end for the lord and his family, and a long stretch of bare stone floor for the rest of the guests, leading to a fireplace big enough to cook an ox on a spit.

There were no longer any tables or benches, but near the dais there was a large round hole in the floor, with a hinged cover made of one thick slab of rock lying flat at its side.

Ten paces away from the hole, nearer the fireplace, stood a tall stone carving. Pearl stepped softly over to it.

It was a throne: a throne built on a column, with rough steps, no more than footholds, curving up and round to the huge seat on the top. It was the height of two tall men, and only a little wider at the base than at the top.

Its rough edges and solid height reminded Pearl of the rock stacks carved by waves off the Scottish coast. It had been hacked from one massive boulder. All the way up the column, jagged mountain peaks had been scraped into the stone, but they looked like scars rather than decoration. She touched the rock with one finger. It was cold. The sun never reached in here.

The Earl grabbed everyone's torches and jammed them into brackets round the walls. Then he clambered onto the dais, turned to face the floor of the hall and opened his arms wide. Pearl moved away from the pillar and stood quietly in a dark corner. After letting Thomas have his way at Swanhaugh Towers, the Earl was now taking charge.

"Swanhaugh. Observe the oubliette." He pointed at the hole in the floor. "From the French word *oublier*, to forget, because the people inside were forgotten. One of our ancestors, one of the lords of Landlaw Hold, was an unforgiving man. He liked to drop those who offended him down there, and let them hear the feasts above as they starved below. We've swept it out for you."

"For me?" the Laird croaked.

"We can't have you wandering loose in our mountains with your nasty bloodlore. I can't take complete control until you're totally defeated. I'm impressed with Thomas's green reed rope, but it wouldn't last more than a day, would it? So we're going to bind you into the foundations of Landlaw Hold."

"You can't!"

"I can, Swanhaugh, I can."

"But I'll fade away in there."

"Don't worry, you will be fed. Most days."

"I mean, I'll fade away without the sky to soar in. I'm a creature of the air, not of burrows and dens. Horsburgh, my cousin, please don't do this to me."

"You lost, Swanhaugh. I won. Will you jump, or shall I get my strong right arm," he gestured at Thomas, "to throw you in?"

"I will jump," the Laird said in a strained voice, but with his head high.

He stepped to the edge and glanced down, then turned to the triplets. "I gave you a gift, children. Perhaps it will save us all," and he leapt into the hole. Pearl held her breath until she heard a dull thump.

Thomas flipped his staff over in his hands, like a sergeant major tossing a baton on parade. As the staff turned in the air, the lid of the oubliette lifted up on its hinge and crashed down to cover the hole.

The Earl rubbed his hands together and nodded at Thomas, who started to twist his staff.

But Jasper stepped forward. "Hold on, sir. Hold on a minute. How long is he going to be down there?"

The Earl didn't answer, but Thomas said in an offhand voice, "As long as you three are up here, your power will keep him down there."

He swung his staff in wider circles, and Pearl noticed the huge rock carving starting to move. She rushed from her corner to drag the girls out of the way and called Jasper to join them against the wall, as the tall chair scraped round the stone floor.

Thomas twirled his staff, and the throne spun round the oubliette like a leaf caught in a whirlpool, grinding smaller and smaller circles, until it settled on top of the trapdoor.

The Earl jumped heavily off the dais, and Pearl stepped back into the shadows. As he strode towards the triplets, she noticed a narrow door in the far corner of the hall. She started to edge towards it.

"That was a little unpleasant, but now we get to have fun," the Earl shouted jovially. "You three are going to sing me a crown."

"Then we'll go home?" sniffed Ruby.

"And the Laird too?" asked Jasper anxiously.

The Earl laughed. "My dear children, I give you my word that you will go home when the Laird goes home. Oh yes. At exactly the same time."

Pearl thought the Earl's vague answer must have satisfied Ruby, because she stuffed her snotty hanky up her sleeve and stopped sniffling. But it hadn't stopped Emmie's questioning gaze flying all around the hall.

Jasper was walking uncertainly towards the stone throne over the oubliette when Thomas called to him, "Jasper, can you give me a hand?"

Pearl was still moving towards the narrow door, but Thomas marched past her, grasped the handle and yanked the door open. Over his shoulder Pearl saw wooden shelves and a stone wall. A cupboard. She sighed, and looked round for other possible ways out.

Thomas jammed the cupboard door open with his heel and lifted a teetering pile of wide stone bowls off a high shelf. "They're very heavy, Jasper. Do you think you can manage a couple?"

"I'm sure I can." Jasper trotted towards Thomas, all his doubts gone now he was being useful.

Pearl counted as the boys brought out twenty-one bowls and arranged them in a circle round the throne.

Then Thomas fetched a bundle of kindling from a heap under the chimney. He twisted handfuls of wood slivers into bonfire shapes, and laid one in each bowl.

Emmie and Jasper watched him, fascinated. Ruby stood nearby, looking occasionally at the locked door. Pearl kept out of the way, hoping for a moment when she could intervene.

Soon Thomas had built pyramids of kindling in every bowl. "Shall I light the fires now, my lord, or wait until you're seated?"

"Light them now, my boy, light them now." The Earl beamed at his grandson then turned to the triplets. "Thomas is just lighting a few fires for us: fires to give light so we can see what we're doing, and warmth so you little dears don't get cold while you sing me a song. Shall we see if you can link your hands round the bottom of this throne?"

Before Pearl could move, the Earl shoved the triplets round the base of the rock chair and ordered them to hold hands in a circle. They had to stretch their arms as far as they would go to reach all the way round, then the Earl checked that each handclasp was firm.

"Well done, well done. It would have been easier in a couple of years when your arms were longer, but as the Laird tried to steal you today, we just had to move everything forward.

"Ready, Thomas?"

"Just a couple more, Grandfather."

Pearl watched as Thomas used a torch to light the small fires in a wide circle round the triplets, who were in a tight circle round the base of the pillar.

The Earl eased Jasper and Ruby's hands apart so he could step onto the stone carving, and barked an order to close the circle again. He didn't climb up, he just stopped and waited on the lowest carved foothold.

Pearl saw Emmie whisper quickly to her brother and sister. Pearl was sure that neither Thomas, with his attention on the fires, nor the Earl, balancing on the carved stone, noticed that when Jasper and Ruby closed the circle again, they held each other by their sleeves not their hands.

Then all the fires were lit. And suddenly it began.

Chapter 28

The Earl ascended the throne, climbing with slow steps that looked regal but were probably an attempt not to slip on the narrow footholds.

Once he had sat down and thumped his huge hands on his wide thighs, he called to the circle of triplets at his feet, "Sing me a crown! Sing me a link to these mountains!"

He closed his eyes.

Pearl stood against the wall, not sure, even after a day of seeing music move mountains, what harm this request for a song could do to the triplets.

Thomas sang a note, and Jasper repeated it. Then Thomas sang a phrase, and Emmie and Ruby copied it. Thomas moved away, as the triplets picked up the music for themselves and started creating their own harmonies and lyrics. Pearl still couldn't grasp the words, couldn't even remember them from one moment to the next, but she got a sense of heat and forging and metal and jewels and swirling endless circles. As he listened, the Earl's face glowed with victory and pride.

Pearl, watching from outside the ring of burning bowls, saw that when the melody moved round the circle of singers, the bowls, balanced on their bases on the stone floor, started to spin. As the song speeded up, the bowls spun faster.

The base of each fire was being pulled round in a circle as the bowl turned, while the length of the flames tried to burn straight upwards. So the flames were twisting and whirling around each other, making patterns like plaits of hair or tartan ribbons.

As the bowls spun even faster, the flames were flung higher, swirling into pillars of fire. At the tip of each pillar, little sparks and flames were torn off to burn in the air.

Pearl stared at the fires, sure she should be coming up with a plan, taking some action. But watching the flames dance and feeling the tiredness in her legs and back, she slid down to sit against the wall. Perhaps the right moment would come soon.

The song grew in intensity and volume. Emmie was leading, Jasper and Ruby's voices dancing round her.

The Earl demanded, "Sing a crown of fire to celebrate my power! Sing a crown of jewels to link me to these rocks! The flame crown will only burn tonight, but so long as you three stones stand here in a circle of song, the crown and the power will be mine for ever. Forever!"

"Forever?" Pearl repeated in a whisper. The triplets had to stay here forever?

"Forever?" she asked more loudly.

She pulled her gaze away from the flames, dragged herself up the wall and staggered out from the shadows.

"Forever?" she shouted over the sound of the music and the roaring of the fires.

"Of course, forever," bellowed the Earl, his eyes still closed. "For us to control the mountains, they must be a crown for ever. Destiny is always for ever!"

Emmie, Ruby and Jasper were still singing, eyes closed, mouths wide. They didn't seem to be listening to anything except each other, flinging notes back and forward.

"Forever!" Pearl turned to Thomas, who was leaning against the opposite wall, staff held loosely in his left hand.

"Did you know you were bringing them here forever?"

He met her eyes steadily. He nodded.

Pearl needed to be sure. "All day, you knew they would be trapped here forever?"

"It was necessary. It's their destiny."

"It wouldn't have been their destiny if you'd said no, if you'd refused to hunt them down."

"It is their destiny to be here," Thomas insisted.

"It won't be their destiny if they stop singing right now."

"They can't stop. It's too late ..."

He gestured upwards.

The tips of the flames, ripped off by the fires' twisting, were being drawn into the centre of the circle, joining together above the Earl's head, creating a jagged and flickering crown of fire.

Pearl guessed when that crown settled on the Earl's head, the ceremony would be complete, and the triplets would be trapped here forever.

She swung round to step between the fires, and pull their hands apart. But Thomas stood in front of her, swinging his staff as he had done that morning at the gate, blocking her way.

"No! Let me past!"

She dodged left, but he was quicker than she was, with a longer reach. He laughed as she dodged right, then left again. His arm and the stick were always there before her. Pearl was trapped on the other side of the fires as her family sung themselves into a crown forever.

Suddenly, in one beat, in one note, the song changed. With a discordant shriek, Emmie stopped the fires' motion dead. She leapt high into the air, flying right through the crown, kicking the points of flame apart, dragging Ruby and Jasper with her.

The children couldn't let go of each other's hands, but the weak bond at Ruby and Jasper's sleeves ripped apart. Now Emmie sang not of fires and circles, but of flying. Her notes swung higher and higher, passing her power and skill to her brother and sister, so they weren't dangling from her hands but floating and swooping with her.

The Earl yelled in anger and drew his horn from his jacket.

Thomas turned his back on Pearl and rushed to the base of the throne.

Emmie, Ruby and Jasper stopped singing. There was silence, apart from the hissing of flame and the whistle of breath.

The two Horsburghs stared at the three children bobbing above them in a line.

Emmie laughed down at them. "Thanks for

the power you let me gather when we did the Laird's gardening. Had you forgotten I could do that, Thomas, or did my sweet smiles and stupid questions make you think I was your servant already?"

Thomas shook his head. "You can do your flying circus tricks with a small handful of power, Emerald, but you can't protect yourself from the force of our lorefasts. You certainly can't protect Ruby and Jasper."

The Earl put the bull's horn to his lips, aiming its dark oval at Jasper. Thomas pointed the staff at Ruby.

"Come down now, and we'll just go back to the start." Thomas's voice was as gentle as his gesture was threatening. "Come down now, and no one will get hurt."

"No. We won't." Emmie spoke softly, but everyone heard her. "We don't want to be your tools. Let us all go now, and neither of *you* will get hurt."

The Earl laughed, clambering down the throne to join Thomas at its base. "How could you hurt us?"

"Because I found the keystone. Because I stored the music of the mountains. Because I already have a lorefast of my own."

Pearl understood before anyone else. She thrust her hands in her pockets and threw handkerchiefs and pencils and string and ribbons on the floor. Did she still have it? Or had it been lost on the journey, during the rocking horse ride to the castle or the swans' attack on the ballroom or the balancing act on the rippling grass?

"I have a lorefast of my own," Emmie repeated. "Pearl? The flint, please."

As Pearl found the arrowhead in the last pocket, Emmie sang a high sharp note to rip her hands from her siblings' grasp, then shouted, "Throw it to me!"

But Thomas had understood too; he was already standing in front of Pearl. Before she could lift her hand to throw the flint, he grabbed her wrist.

"Drop it," he ordered.

The Earl blew his horn straight at Jasper, flinging the boy across the hall, crushing him against the wall, dropping him to the floor.

"Thomas!" Pearl pleaded.

The Earl blew his horn again, as Emmie and Ruby flew in circles above him, trying to avoid the ringing blasts.

"The flint!" yelled Emmie.

The Earl was whirling on the spot, his broad face red and shiny. "If you won't crown me, changeling, then you won't get out of here alive!" He blew again and again.

Thomas ignored the noise behind him and gripped Pearl harder.

"Let go of me," said Pearl, making a heart-bursting effort to stay calm.

Thomas shook his head.

"Look at Jasper!"

They both looked at the crumpled boy on the floor. They both looked back at the flint in her hand.

"Thomas. Let go of my wrist."

"No. This is my destiny."

Ruby screamed, as the Earl's echoing notes smashed her against the rafters. Thomas and Pearl looked up. Ruby fell out of the air, but Emmie caught her and started dodging about the roof space with her sister clutched in her arms.

"Thomas, he is going to kill her. He is going to kill them all."

"This was their choice." His voice was still strong and calm, but his eyes flicked fast between the girls struggling above him, the boy on the floor and the flint in Pearl's fist. "It was their choice to fight against their destiny."

"No, Thomas." Pearl remembered the last time he'd had a firm grip on her wrist and she had forced him to make a choice.

Chapter 29

Over the noise of the battle, Pearl spoke clearly and slowly. "No, Thomas, this is *your* choice."

Thomas's eyes widened, and the pressure on her wrist relaxed.

In that moment, Pearl ripped her wrist out of his grasp and yelled, "EMMIE!" Using all her hunter's skill at hitting a moving target, she flung the flint to Emmie, who let Ruby fall as she caught it, then swooped under her sister to hold her again.

Emmie swerved in the air to avoid another horn blast and dived over to Pearl, dropping a limp Ruby into her arms.

Then she flew to the rafters and held the flint, her lorefast, in both hands. And she began to sing, creating a fearful and furious music, but with no time to form words.

First she dropped a jangling rockfall of sharp notes onto Thomas's head. He collapsed to the floor, letting go of his staff. Pearl kicked it aside, so when he sat up groaning he couldn't reach it.

The Earl screamed as he saw his grandson fall, and gulped deep breath after deep breath to blow notes like storm-winds at Emmie.

She was battered by the air, her hair coiling round her head, her petticoats billowing round her legs. Pearl, standing guard between Thomas and his lorefast, found herself thinking that Emmie should wear boys' trousers to fly in public.

Emmie's flying was so fast and precise, she was able to ride the Earl's blasts of sound or dive under them.

The Earl's face was turning purple as he strained to get enough breath to match Emmie's speed.

His thumping notes stopped for a second while he took a deep screeching chestful of air. Emmie swooped down and flung a cascade of noise at him that buried him under invisible power. His horn was torn from his lips and clattered to the floor, leaving him empty-handed as Emmie stood on the air in front of him.

Emmie pointed the flint at the Earl and began at last to sing words again. She sang a song brimming with anger: anger at being hunted and caught and compelled; anger at the bruised bodies of her brother and sisters; anger at being dragged from the schoolroom into someone else's war.

The Earl shook in the waves of power, unable to get away, his head lolling back on a slack neck.

Pearl couldn't move towards Emmie because of the drooping weight of Ruby in her arms, so she opened her mouth to yell, "*No!*"

But Emmie had made her choice.

She turned her back suddenly on the Earl, letting him fall to the ground, and flew straight at the stone throne, blasting the pillar off the oubliette and shattering it into a thousand pieces of gravel.

She screamed the trapdoor open, and sang a

rising staircase of song until the Laird limped out, struggling free of the green reed rope.

Emmie hovered above the wreck of the feasting hall.

The air stopped shaking.

Pearl, arms trembling, placed Ruby on the floor beside Jasper. Both of them were breathing and Ruby was already moving weakly.

The Earl, Thomas and the Laird were all slumped on the ground.

"Now who will rule the mountains?" asked the Laird hoarsely.

Emmie floated down to perch on the remains of the stone throne.

"I will."

Chapter 30

"I will look after the mountains," Emmie said in her high clear voice.

"You!" spluttered the Earl.

"Me. You both created me, you both gave me your powers, but then you put me in a family where I could learn *my* way of using power, not yours.

"So I will listen to the mountains, Ruby and Jasper will listen to the Chayne lands, and the Swanns and Horsburghs will listen to your own lands. I will watch over both of you from the summits, and if you use bloodlore, or conspire to get more power than you need, then I will see and I will come down ..."

She slashed the flint through the air, and the fires in the bowls flared into roaring fingers, reaching out for the Earl and the Laird, who scrambled away against the wall.

Emmie cut the fires back down, then smiled sweetly.

The Laird took out a silver flask, drank a large mouthful and offered it to the Earl, who accepted.

Pearl wiped Ruby and Jasper's faces with a hanky she'd dropped on the floor when she was hunting through her pockets. Ruby was bashed and bruised, but not crying. Jasper groaned himself awake and asked, "Is everyone else alright?" Pearl nodded, hoping it was true.

Emmie jumped down from the cairn of rubble and trotted over to her family. Pearl stood up, amazed to see that Emmie was still shorter than her.

"Thank you," Emmie hugged her. "Thank you for staying with us."

"But why didn't you tell me the flint had so much power in it?"

"If I'd told you, you'd have guarded it closely and kept checking your pockets. Then Thomas would have noticed. Anyway, I knew you would get it here safely; you never lose anything out of those pockets. And Thomas never guessed."

They both looked over at Thomas. He was sitting on the floor, far away from his grandfather, head tipped back against the wall. His lorefast lay abandoned by a smouldering bowl.

Pearl crossed the hall, picked up the staff and walked over to Thomas. As she carried it, she heard the pearl jumping lightly inside the shell. She offered the staff to Thomas. He ignored her.

She sat down near him. She didn't say anything.

Eventually, he spoke. "I was weak. I made a sentimental choice. I should have been strong. I should have remembered my ambition and my mission, and not let anyone get in my way. I should have held on."

He looked over at Emmie, talking quietly to Jasper and Ruby.

"But I think the mountains are in better hands, aren't they?"

"I hope so," said Pearl. Then she laughed, briefly. "Maybe this was everyone's destiny after all."

Thomas stared at her. "Do you believe that?"

"No. We all had to make choices, and it could have gone wrong so many times on the journey, couldn't it?"

"It has gone wrong for me."

Pearl shook her head and tapped the shell on his staff very gently. She heard the pearl shift and roll inside. "You have the ancient lorefast now. You did earn it. You can go and save the world, if you still think you're the right person to do it."

Thomas stood up and brushed dust off his trousers. "I should go home. The horses will be reaching the stables soon, and the grooms won't like unsaddling rocking horses."

Pearl nodded. "We should go home too. Mother will have sent out our groom and gardener to hunt for us when we didn't turn up for supper."

She held out the staff to him again. He took it, and looking at the lorefast rather than Pearl, he said, "Perhaps we could go hunting together again? You could teach me how to read the land as well as listen to it."

"What would we hunt?"

"Deer or pheasant." He looked straight at her. "Not swans or rocking horses."

"Nor children?"

He glanced over at Emmie, Ruby and Jasper.

"Never again, no matter who tells me it's my destiny." Thomas almost smiled. Then he turned and walked away, carrying his staff.

"Let's go home," Pearl called to the triplets as

she stood up and stretched. "The stars will give us enough light to hike through the Grey Men's Grave, and we'll get home before the sun comes up. I've worked out a quicker route than the one marked on Peter's maps."

"Couldn't we use Emmie's power to fly home?" asked Ruby.

"No." Emmie curled her fingers round the flint. "The power isn't really mine. It belongs to the land, and I don't want to waste it. Not on a shortcut home. I'll keep it for more important things."

"Like what?" asked Jasper, helping Ruby to her feet and keeping an arm round her shoulders.

Emmie watched Thomas as he unlocked the door and left the feasting hall. "I don't know yet. Let's follow Thomas. I still have a lot to learn from him, but don't dare tell him that."

The Chayne children walked out of the castle together, leaving two old men behind them.

Pearl looked up at the dark spaces where the mountains hid during the night, and knew that she didn't need her mother's permission or her father's company to make them her own now.

"I'm hungry," said Jasper, as they crossed the narrow path under the arrowslits.

"We're all hungry!" laughed Pearl. "But we won't be for long. Mother sent me to fetch you for breakfast, and we're only a day late."